Outwitting the DEVIL

Outwitting the DEVIL
JACK TALES
From Wise County Virginia

Edited by
Charles L. Perdue, Jr.

Ancient City Press
Santa Fe, New Mexico

International Standard Book Number:
Clothbound 0-941270-43-2
Paperback 0-941270-42-4
Library of Congress Catalogue Number:
87-071657

Second Edition

Book Design by Mary Powell
Cover Design by Stephen Tongier

Printed in the United States of America

Both the tales and "Old Jack and the New Deal" originally appeared in *Appalachian Journal* Vol. 14, No. 2 (Winter 1987), and are reprinted with permission.

Cover: Nancy (Old Granny) Shores on the Mullins Fork of Bold Camp, Wise County, Virginia. Photo from Luther F. Addington, *The Story of Wise County (Virginia)*, and used with permission of Mrs. Luther F. Addington.

Cover: Coverlet Detail. Woven wool coverlet made ca. 1819 by Liza Jan Weddell of Floyd Co., VA, for her daughter, Susan Vancil. This item was owned in 1937 by Mrs. John Dowdell of Sawtelle, CA, who was a great-great-granddaughter of Liza Jan Weddell. The plate for this coverlet was rendered by Index artist Cornelius Christoffels. Index of American Design (SoCAL-te-102b); National Gallery of Art, Washington.

Frontispiece: John Martin Kilgore and family of Wise, Virginia. Photo from the James Taylor Adams Papers, John Cook Wyllie Library, Clinch Valley College, Wise, Virginia.

Spacer motifs: Applique "Friendship" Quilt. Pattern also known as a "Baltimore Bride's Quilt." It was originally made by a Mrs. Kelly, ca. 1830 in Middlesex Co., VA. The quilt was owned in 1942 by Miss Hilda Hodgers of Ruark, Middlesex Co., VA, who was a granddaughter of Mrs. Kelly. Miss Hodgers lent the quilt to "the Middlesex County Museum, a Unit of the Virginia Art Project, and [it] was recorded there" by artist Mary Ann Burton. Index of American Design (VA-te-17); National Gallery of Art, Washington.

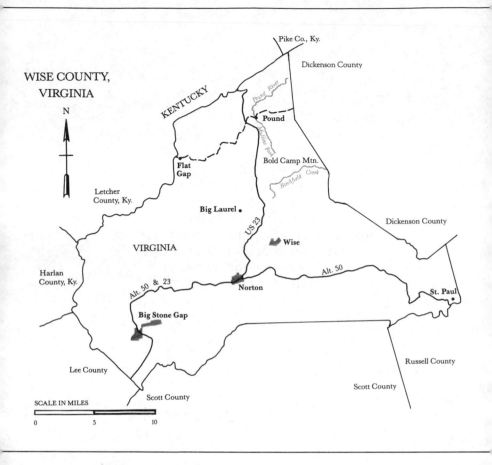

WISE COUNTY, VIRGINIA

N

Pike Co., Ky.

Dickenson County

KENTUCKY

Pound River

Pound

Indian Fork

Flat Gap

Bold Camp Mtn.

Letcher County, Ky.

Birchfield Creek

Big Laurel •

Dickenson County

US 23

Wise

VIRGINIA

Alt. 50

Harlan County, Ky.

Alt. 50 & 23

Norton

St. Paul

Big Stone Gap

Russell County

Lee County

Scott County

Scott County

SCALE IN MILES

0   5   10

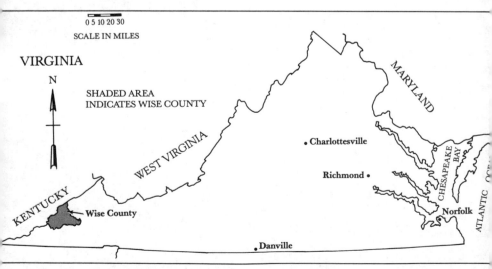

0 5 10 20 30

SCALE IN MILES

VIRGINIA

N

SHADED AREA
INDICATES WISE COUNTY

MARYLAND

WEST VIRGINIA

• Charlottesville

CHESAPEAKE BAY

Richmond •

ATLANTIC OCEAN

KENTUCKY

Wise County

Norfolk

• Danville

Contents

Acknowledgements

For her assistance with the James Taylor Adams Papers we are grateful to the late Rosemary P. Mercure, former head of Public Services, and to the rest of the staff at the John Cook Wyllie Library, Clinch Valley College, Wise, Virginia. Former Virginia Writers' Project folklore collector Emory Hamilton in Wise was invaluable for sharing with us his recollections of the Project and of his associate James Taylor Adams. We also appreciate the time taken by James Taylor Adams, II, to speak with us about his father's life and work. In addition, further contextual information was provided by various communications with folkorist Herbert Halpert and through an interview with Richard Chase.

Edmund Berkeley, Jr., Michael F. Plunket, Gregory A. Johnson, and the staff of the Manuscripts Department, Alderman Library, University of Virginia, have all gone beyond the call of duty over the years that we have been working on the New Deal materials. We wish also to extend our appreciation to Joseph C. Hickerson and Gerald E. Parsons, Jr., at the Archive of Folk Culture, Library of Congress; Richard Crawford and the staff at the National Archives; and the diligent and courteous staff of the Archives Branch, Virginia State Library, Richmond.

The Index of American Design plates used in this book were obtained from the National Gallery, Washington, D.C., through the gracious efforts of Index Assistant Curators Laurie Weitzenkorn and Charles Ritchie, and Ira Bartfield, Chief of Photographic Services at the Gallery. Some of the photographs in the book are used with the kind permission of Mrs. Luther F. Addington of Wise, Virginia.

Nancy J. Martin-Perdue assisted equally in the research upon which this book is based. She also critiqued the work in its various stages and made numerous suggestions for improvement— most of which were followed.

Finally, we wish to acknowledge the assistance of our longtime friend and associate in New Deal research, Marta Weigle.

Introduction

Jack tales are American versions of European Märchen (or fairy-tales) and usually involve the exploits and adventures of a young hero, Jack. Readers will likely be familiar with the European tale of "Jack and the Beanstalk," but they may not be aware that a version of this tale survived in oral tradition in America. Characteristically, the American Jack steals from the giant a gun and a knife, rather than the moneybags and the hen that lays the golden eggs common in English versions. In many of the tales Jack, through naive good luck, magic gifts, and help from sympathetic people or animals, does good deeds for a variety of folks from beggars to kings and usually ends up with the money or the princess (sometimes the Devil's daughter), or both.

Jack tales were fairly common in America in the eighteenth century but, like other forms of oral literature, gradually came to be replaced by written forms such as the novel, the romance, almanacs, and newspapers. Still, the stories survived in areas and among people with a strong oral tradition: the Ozarks, the Sea Islands off the Carolinas and Georgia, ethnic enclaves such as the French of Missouri or the Italians of West Virginia, and among Southern Mountain people in western North Carolina and Wise County, Virginia.

Wise County resident James Taylor Adams, who gathered most of the tales presented in this book, knew about Jack tales, but their collection was spurred through the efforts of Richard Chase, a puppeteer, recreation worker, and professional tale-teller. In 1935, Chase had been working at a teachers' conference in Raleigh, North Carolina, conducting a workshop on folksongs when a member of his audience told him about the Jack tale tradition in Western North Carolina. Chase shortly began to collect, publish, and perform these tales, making them available to a popular audience.

In 1940 Chase learned of the Jack tale tradition in Wise County, Virginia, and the following year he organized a project through the WPA's Virginia Writers' Project to collect them. By the close of the VWP in June of 1942, nineteen tales (twenty-eight variants) had been collected by James Taylor Adams and James M. Hylton, workers on the Virginia Writers' Project.

For the first time, these Wise County tales are presented here in their original form as collected by Adams and Hylton. They make an interesting comparison to the well-known, popular versions of Jack tales compiled by Richard Chase in *The Jack Tales* (Houghton-Mifflin, 1943). It was public performance that concerned Chase primarily, and he freely combined and altered the versions that he and others had collected in order to create forms that he felt would be more appealing to his audience.

The tale texts in this work are followed by "Old Jack and the New Deal," a discussion of Jack tales, the Virginia Writers' Project, and the role of Richard Chase in the collection of Jack tales and other folklore in Wise County, Virginia. A note on the federal relief projects represented in texts and illustrations is also appended.

READERS GUIDE

It is beyond the scope of this book to provide detailed analyses of these tale texts or to present a detailed list of motifs and analogues. However, where I could determine the tale type I have given that and for several tales not easily typed I have given the primary motif(s). In this endeavor I have utilized Antti Aarne and Stith Thompson's *The Types of the Folktale: A Classification and Bibliography*, (Helsinki: FF Communications No. 184, 1964) and Ernest W. Baughman, *Type and Motif-Index of the Folktales of England and North America* (The Hague: Mouton & Co., 1966). The reader might consult Herbert Halpert's copious notes included as an appendix in Chase's *The Jack Tales*. For more recently collected Jack tales see Leonard W. Roberts' work in Kentucky: *South from Hell-fer-Sartin* (Berea, KY: Council of Southern Mountains, Inc., 1964); *Old Greasybeard: Tales from the Cumberland Gap* (Detroit: Folklore Associates, 1969); and *Sang Branch Settlers: Folk-songs and Tales of a Kentucky Mountain Family* (Austin: University of Texas Press (American Folklore Society), 1974). I will use brief citations for Richard Chase's books; see End Note 38 for full citations. In presenting these tales the only editing I have done is to silently correct the most obvious typographical errors.

The Tales

I-A / *The Endless Tale*

ONE TIME THEY WAS A KING who had a beautiful daughter. He put out that he'd give her for a wife to the man who'd tell him the longest tale. There was one condition and that was if one failed after he started that he'd get his head cut off.

Several men come and tried to win the girl, but they failed to please the king and had to stop because they couldn't keep on with the tale he had their heads cut off.

They was a boy named Jack and he heard about it an' he said he'd try. The king told him to go ahead, but if he stopped he'd get his head cut off. So Jack started in to tell his tale.

He said that one time they was another king and that he took one-tenth of every thing his people raised for tax. He built a big house in the middle of his kingdom and filled it with rice the people had raised. Well a rat started gnawin' at one corner and finally it got so hit could get in an' hit got one grain of rice an' carried it out. The next day hit went in an' got one more grain. The next day hit went in an' got one more grain. The next day hit went in an' got one more grain. The next day hit went in an' got one more grain. Jack just kept right on goin' over an' over with that for a whole day. The king was so tired of hearing about the rat goin' in the house an' getting one more grain that he told him to shet up he could have his daughter.

Collected by James Taylor Adams on December 22, 1941, from Mrs. Bethel Lee Adams of Big Laurel, Virginia. She learned it from her grandmother, Mrs. Celia Banks. This is tale type 2301, "Corn Carried away Grain at a Time."

I-B / The Longest Tale

ONE TIME THERE WAS A KING who offered his daughter to the man that would tell him the longest tale. The girl was very beautiful and would be the queen [when] her father died. So a lot of young men tried making up long tales. Dozens and dozens of them went in and told the king a tale. At last there came in a boy from the backwoods country and he started in telling his tale. Said that there once was a rich landlord and he built a big granary to horde his rents in wheat in. He had it full and to overflowing, but a locust gnawed through and got a grain, then it went in and got another grain and another grain and another grain and another grain and another grain. "Stop," said the king, "Is that all you are going to tell?" "Sure," said the boy. "That's all the locust done. Just one grain after another. Won't you let me go on and finish the tale. He's only got out a few grains now, and the granary has thousands of bushels you know." "No," said the king. "I've heard a plenty. Go ahead and take my daughter."

Collected by James Taylor Adams on December 23, 1941, from John Edwards of St. Paul, Virginia, who heard it from his grandfather John Edwards about 1890.

1-C / *The Tale Without an End*

ONE TIME THERE WAS A GREAT KING and he norated through-out his kingdom that the man who could tell him an endless tale could have his daughter for a wife and be the king when he was dead. Several young men came and tried to tell a tale with-out an end, but they all run out of something to tell. At last a boy named Jack came in and told the king a tale.

Jack told the king that once there was a king who gathered all the wheat that his people had raised and put it in a big gra-nary and was going to doll it out as he seen fit. But a rat cut a hole in the wall and went in and got one grain of the wheat. The next day it went in and got one more grain. The next day it went in and got one more grain. Jack just kept telling about the rat going in and out until the king couldn't stand it any longer and he told him to hush and he could have the girl.

Aldred B. Franklin was present when Mrs. Bethel Lee Adams told THE ENDLESS TALE [see 1-A above]. He said "I've heard grandma Robbins tell that, but she called it THE TALE WITHOUT AN END, and hit went like this . . . "

2 / *Fourteen*

ONE TIME THERE WAS AN AWFUL LAZY BOY. His name was Jack. He was overgrown, six foot tall and weighed about two hundred. But he wouldn't do a thing but just lay around. In the summer time he would set around in the shade of a tree and slap at flies that bothered him. One day he piled up the flies he killed and found he'd killed fourteen. So he got some poke ber-ries and painted on his forehead:
"KILLED FOURTEEN AND WOUNDED TWENTY-EIGHT."

A giant who lived in the hills back of the country where lazy Jack lived came along and seed the sign. Now he was jeal-ous for he'd only killed seven men and wounded fourteen, just half the number Jack had painted on his forehead, and of course he thought Jack had killed fourteen men and wounded twenty-eight. So he got Jack to go home with him. Said to hisself he might come in handy. Anyway a strong feller like him can do a lot of work. But Jack, who the giant called "Fourteen," wouldn't strike a tap. Just laid around the giant's cave and let him wait on him. And the old giant was afraid to ask him to do anything. He was afraid of him with his reputation. But one day he ventured to tell him to take the wagon and hawl in a load of wood. Fourteen went out and looked at the wagon. Hit was so heavy he couldn't even move it. So he went back in and said, "I wouldn't fool to bring wood in on a little old wagon like that. If hit's all right with you I'll just toss it up to my brother who lives in the clouds and let him bring us a load that is a load." The giant was scared. He said, "No, no, Fourteen, don't do that. I'll get the wood myself." And he did.

So hit went on awhile and the giant thought he'd get some use out of him so he told him to take that big bucket out there and fetch in a little water. So Fourteen he went out and found the bucket. Oh hit was so heavy he couldn't budge it. So he studied and went back in and said to the giant: "Where's the mattock?" "What do you want with the mattock," asked the giant. "Oh," said Fourteen, "I wouldn't fool to carry water in a little old bucket like that. Get me the mattock and I'll just dig the well up and carry hit in." Well, that scared the old giant worse 'n ever an' he said, "Oh, no, Fourteen, just let hit go. I'll carry in the water." And he did.

So hit went on for about a month. The old giant began to suspicion Fourteen. So he struck on a plan to try him out for strength. So one evenin' he said, "Fourteen, in the mornin' we go up yanner to that big white oak and try our strength out by seein' which one can jam his fist in it the furderest." Fourteen said all right, but he was into [it] then. He didn't know what to do. So that night he laid awake all night trying to plan out some way of foolin' the giant and keepin' his reputation. Along about four o'clock he thought of a big auger he'd seed around the giant's cave. So he just slipped out of bed and found it and went up to the big white oak and bored a hole straight through it and then put the bark back over both holes.

Well the next mornin' the old giant was out early and hollered for Fourteen to "come on an' les go." So they went up to the big tree and Fourteen told the giant that hit was his idea, his tree and he was the oldest, so for him to try fust. The giant drawed back and "kerslam!" His fist sunk up into the solid body of the tree for six inches. Fourteen looked like he thought he might be beat, but he told the giant that he'd get around on the other side and he did and he rammed his fist in at one side and out at the other through the auger hole. And the giant was convinced that Fourteen was all he claimed to be and he was scareder of him than ever.

Now the giant was a-courtin' the King's daughter. So he took Fourteen with him one day when he went to see the girl. They went in and the Giant, "Killed seven and wounded fourteen," he boasted. Fourteen he said, "Killed fourteen and wounded twenty-eight." So the King heard that and he wanted his gal to quit the giant and marry Fourteen, but she didn't like Fourteen and druther had the giant. Then the King said I'll tell you what I'll do. My daughter can sleep between you and the one she is facin' when I come in she'll marry. So Fourteen he studied out a plan to git the gal. He went out and ketched him a skunk and fetched up pretty close the house and tied hit in the path. So they went to bed and the gal she laid facin' the giant. But along in the night Fourteen whispered to the giant: "You know we left the gate open as we come in. If the King finds it open he [will] kill us both. Better get up and go shet it." So the giant was afeared of Fourteen and he got up and went out to shet the gate and run over the skunk and when he come back he was a sight in the world to smell. The gal tried to lay facin' him, but she just couldn't stand it, and in a little while she turned over and faced Fourteen. She was lyin' that way when the King come in. But she wasn't satisfied with that and she bagged the King to give the giant one more test. Well, he said he would. Said they was a big lion loose and the one that brought in his right fore foot fust could marry his daughter.

So they struck out. Fourteen told the giant to go up one

hollow and he's go up the other. They hadn't gone fer tell Fourteen heard a fight start an' and seed the giant a comin' and the
lion right after him nippity tuck. He scaled a tree an' the giant
didn't see him. Right under the tree the lion ketched up with the
giant and the fight started in ernest[sic]. At last the giant killed
the lion, but he was so give out that he just fell over dead to the
world for a right smart bit. Then Fourteen crawled down and
slipped over to the dead lion and cut off hit's right fore foot and
ran to the King with it. And the King let him marry the gal and
the last time I was through there they was a-gettin' along pretty
well.

*Collected by James Taylor Adams on January 21, 1942, from James W.
Hays of St. Paul, Virginia. He learned it from his father about 1890. This
is Type 1640, "The Brave Tailor." For Chase's version see* American Folk
Tales, JACK AND OLD STRONGMAN.

3-A / *Jack and the Bull*

ONE TIME THERE WAS A LITTLE BOY. And his name was Jack.
And he was a bound boy. He was bound to an old man who
was rich and had lots of land and cattle. The old man liked Jack,
but the old woman hated him. The girls liked Jack very well. But
the old woman somehow just hated Jack.

Jack had to work awful hard. He didn't get anything for his
work only his clothes and what he eat. But the old man liked
Jack and he give Jack a calf and the calf growed up and made a
big fine black bull.

Jack had to go to the pasture and feed the cattle twice every
day. He had to go in the morning and he had to go in the
evening.

The old woman decided she was going to get rid of Jack.
She thought how she would get rid of him. And she decided
she would starve him to death. So she got to getting breakfast
while Jack was gone to feed the cattle of a morning and supper
while he was gone to feed them in the evening. At dinner time

she wouldn't call Jack to dinner at all.

So Jack got to starving nearly to death. He got so weak he just barely could walk. All he had to eat was a few crumbs he would pick up around the kitchen where the old woman threw them out to the chickens.

So Jack was just about to starve to death. One evening he went to the pasture to feed the cattle and he was so weak he could hardly walk and he set down on a rock and began to cry.

Jack's bull saw Jack a crying and he walked over and asked Jack what he was crying about. Jack told him the old woman was a starving him to death; that she would not give him a bite to eat and all he had had in a week was a few crumbs he had picked up in the floor and yard.

The bull told Jack for him not to cry. Just screw off my left horn and you'll find bread and butter; and screw off the right horn and you'll find bread and milk. Jack screwed off the left horn and sure enough there was bread and butter and he screwed off the right horn and there was bread and milk. He eat all he wanted and screwed the horns back on his bull. He kept this up every morning and evening and Jack was getting fat. The old woman noticed it and wondered why he was gaining in flesh when he was not getting anything to eat. She knew he was eating something, so she decided to set a spy to watch him.

Now she had three girls. One was a three-eyed girl; one was a two-eyed girl and the other was a one-eyed girl. So she sent her three-eyed girl to watch Jack when he went to feed and see where he got something to eat. But the three-eyed girl she got sleepy after watching awhile and she laid down in the shade of a tree and went to sleep. Jack screwed off his bull's horn and eat his supper, but the girl was asleep and didn't see him.

So the old woman sent her two-eyed girl to watch next day and she watched a while, didn't see anything and she laid down and went to sleep. Then Jack came and screwed off his bull's horn and eat his supper. The two-eyed girl went back and told her mother she didn't see Jack eat a bite of anything.

The old woman she was mad. She knew he was getting something to eat somewhere and she was going to find out where he was getting it. So the next day she sent her one-eyed girl to watch. And she watched and saw Jack screw off his bull's horns and get his supper and she run home and told her mother about it.

So the old woman knew the only way to get rid of Jack was to get rid of his bull. So she told her old man that she was longing for Jack's bull's melt and that he'd have to kill the bull so she could have his melt to eat. The old man didn't want to kill Jack's bull and he tried to get her to let him kill another bull and let her have his melt. No, she had to have Jack's bull's melt. She was longing for Jack's bull's melt and no other melt would satisfy her. So the old man finally agreed to kill Jack's bull and he told Jack that the old woman was a longing for his bull's melt and he would have to kill him. Jack didn't know what to do. That evening when he went to feed he was a crying. The bull asked him what was the matter and he told him the old woman was a longing for his melt and they were going to kill him and that he would starve to death after he was killed. The bull told Jack not to cry. He said: "Now I won't let nobody come near me but the old woman and you. So you agree to knock me in the head and get her to hold me and when you go to strike me make a mislick and hit her and kill her and then you jump upon my back and I will carry you to safety."

So the next day they sent Jack to get the bull and bring [him] to the house to be killed. He came along peacefully enough. They turned him in the lot around the stable and the old man undertook to get a hold of him to hold. He had ordered Jack to get a big hammer and knock him in the head. But the bull seemed afraid of the old man and would not let him come near him. So the old woman she got to petting him and he stood still. She then laid hold of his horns and hollered to Jack to run and knock him in the head. Jack swung the big hammer and struck the old woman right between the eyes and killed her as dead as a door-nail. Then he sprang on his bull's back and the bull ran out of the lot and away down the road.

They went on and on and on till one day on ahead of them they heard another bull a bellowing. Jack's bull told Jack that

that was a big red bull and that when they met that they would have an awful fight, but that he would finally kill the big red bull. So they went on and after while they saw the big red bull in the road pawing up the ground. Him and Jack's bull locked horns and started to fight; and they fought and fought, while Jack sat on the bank and watched them. Several times he thought the red bull was going to kill his bull, but finally his bull got him down and gored him to death against the bank. Then Jack screwed off his bull's horn and eat his supper, while his bull picked grass by the road. Then they went on their way.

They went on and on and on till one day they heard another bull a bellowing. Jack's bull told Jack that was a big blue bull and that when they met up with him they would have an awful fight, and he would finally kill him, but he would have a harder time with him than he did with the red bull.

So they went on and after a while they saw the big blue bull coming to meet them, bellowing and pawing up the ground. Him and Jack's bull locked horns and they fought and fought and fought, lots of times the big blue bull would have Jack's bull down and he thought he was going to kill him sure, but he would always get up and at last Jack's bull got him down and killed him. Then they eat their supper, Jack from his bull's horn and the bull from grass by the road and they went on their way.

They went on and on and on and one day away on ahead of them they heard another bull a bellowing. He bellowed so loud he shook the ground. Jack's bull told Jack that that was a big white bull and that when they met up with him they would have an awful fight and he would finally kill him. "And you will be left alone, Jack," said his bull, "but don't cry. After the big white bull kills me you skin a piece of skin from the end of my nose to the root of my tail and take it up on the hill and strike three times with it across a hollow log and wish for anything you want and you will get it."

So they went and after a while they saw the big white bull coming to meet them bellowing and pawing up the ground and swinging his head from side to side. Him and Jack's bull locked horns and they fought and fought and fought nearly all day.

Jack's bull had him down several times and Jack thought he was going to kill him, but finally he killed Jack's bull, and after his bull was dead and the big white bull had gone on, Jack got out his pocketknife and skun a piece of skin from the end of his bull's nose to the root of his tail. He couldn't hardly bear to do this and he cried all the time, but finally he got the piece of skin off and he went off up on the hill and there was a big hollow log and Jack took the piece of skin and struck it across the log three times and wished he had a horse, bridle and saddle, and a hundred dollars in money. He looked up the road and there came the finest horse he had even seen with a fine saddle and bridle on it. He went down and climb on the horse's back and there was a pair of saddle pockets across the saddle. He put his hand in them and there was a hundred dollars in money. So he rode off to seek his fortune.

This tale was told to James Taylor Adams by his wife Dicy Adams, of Big Laurel, Virginia, and he "set it down as near as possible in her own words." Dicy learned the tale from her mother, Mrs. Letty Adams Mays, and she says she learned it from her mother Celia Church Adams, whose parents came to Wise County, Virginia from Wilkes County, North Carolina about 1800. This is basically tale Type 511A, "The Little Red Ox," with some minor variations. See Chase, Jack Tales, JACK AND THE BULL.

3-B / *Jack and the Bull*

ONE TIME THERE WAS A PORE BOY. His name was Jack an' he worked fer a rich family. The old man liked Jack, but the old woman jis hated him. She would send Jack to feed the cattle ever time jis about when she got sump'n to eat ready. Jack was jis goin' to skin an' bones. Nearly starved to death.

One day a strange bull come along an' jumped in the field. An' that evenin' when Jack went to feed the cattle he was cryin'. The bull said, "What's the matter, Jack? What are ye cryin' about?" Jack told him the old woman was tryin' to starve him to death an' sent him to feed ever' time when she got sump'n to eat ready.

The bull said, "Don't worry Jack. You jis beat on my right horn an' you find cheese an' bread an' beat on my left horn an' you'll find milk an' butter." So Jack beat on his right horn an' there was all the bread an' cheese he wanted to eat an' he beat on the left horn an' thar was all the milk an' butter he could eat. So he went back to the house feelin' good. An' he begin to pick right up fer he eat that way ever' day.

Wudn't long tell the old woman noticed he was gainin' flash an' she wondered what was the reason. So she had two boys. One was a two-eyed boy an' the other was a three-eyed boy. She sent the two-eyed boy to watch an' see where Jack was gittin' his eatins. Now Jack he was a fiddler. An' when he seed the two-eyed boy thar watchin' him he took his fiddle an' set down upon the bank an' started playin'. He played an' he played tell one eye was played to sleep an' he played an' he played tell the other eye was played to sleep an' then he beat on the bull's horns an' got his supper.

So the two-eyed boy waked up after while an' went back an' told his mother he didn't see a thing. So she sent the three-eyed boy to watch. An' Jack he took his fiddle an' set down on the bank an' started playin'. He played an' he played an' he played one eye to sleep. An' he played an' he played an' he played another eye to sleep. An' he played an' he played an' he played but he couldn't never git the third eye played to sleep. He was gittin' mighty hungry an' he went over an' beat on the bull's horns an' eat his supper an' the three-eyed boy seed him out of the one eye he hadn't played to sleep an' he went back an' told his mammy.

So the next day she told her old man that she was longin' fer that strange bull's liver an' lights an' he'd have to kill him an' git his liver an' lights fer her. He didn't want to do it, but she kept right on an' on. Finally he told Jack he'd have to kill the strange bull an' git his liver an' lights fer his wife. Jack went to the field that evenin' a cryin'. The bull said, "What's wrong now, Jack?" He told him that the old woman had found out where he was gittin' his eatins an' had made up her mind to have his liver an' lights.

The bull told Jack not to worry, that he'd jump on one of the cows an' kill her and they'd git her liver an' lights an' let Jack take 'em to the old woman an' she'd not know the difference. So he did an' Jack took the liver an' lights an' give 'em to the old woman an' then he went back an' the bull told him to climb up on his back an' he'd carry him to safety. An' Jack got up on his back an' they traveled an' traveled on and traveled on.

One mornin' they got up an' the bull looked bothered. Jack axed him what was the matter, an' he told Jack he'd had a bad dream. Said he had dreamed they was goin' along an' met up with a two-headed bull an' him an' the two-headed bull had fit an' fit but that he had finally whuped the two-headed bull.

So they went on an' on an' shore enough that day they met up with a two-headed bull an' Jack got off his bull's back an' crawled up on the bank an' they went to fightin'. They fit an' they fit. Lot o' times Jack thought the ol' two-headed bull was goin' to kill his bull, but finally his bull whuped him. An' [Jack] got on his bull an they went on.

The next mornin' the bull looked more bothered than ever. Jack wanted to know what was the matter. An' he told Jack he'd dreamed they met a three-headed bull an' they had a fight an' he killed him. He tol' Jack 'f they did meet a three-headed bull an' he got killed fer him to skin a strip from the tip of his tail to his head an' take off his horns an' take it with him, an' any time he was in trouble to jis say:

"Tie, strap, tie,
Beat, horns, beat"

an' he would git anything he wanted.

So they went on an' shore enough they met up with a big three-headed bull an' Jack got off of his bull's back an' clomb on the bank an' they started fightin'. They fit an' they fit an' at last the three-headed bull killed his bull an' went on up the road bellowin'. Jack got down an' took out his pocketknife an' skun a strip from the end's his bull's tail to the tip of his nose an' took off his horns an' went on. When he got hungry all he had to do was beat on the horns an' git his eatins.

He went on an' on an' finally one day he stopped at a house where an' old woman lived an' she wanted to hire him to herd sheep for her. He took the job an' all the neighbors told him he couldn't git along with her that she was contrary an' mean. But he worked on tell one day she come out where he was an' said, "Jack, which do you chose, hard gripes or sharp shins." He told her he believed he'd rather have hard gripes. So she jumped on him an' started chokin' him. He hollered out, "Tie, strap, tie, Beat, horns, beat!" An' the strap tied her down an' the horns set in to beatin' her. She couldn't stan' that so she tol' Jack to take 'em off an' she [would] buy him a new suit of clothes. So Jack took 'em off. An' hit went on a few days an' the old woman didn't bother him any more. Then she come out where he was at ag'in an' said, "Jack, which do you chose, hard gripes or sharp shins." Jack said, "Hard gripes." An' she jumped on him ag'in an' begin choking him. He hollered, "Tie, strap, tie, Beat, horns, beat," an' the strap tied her down an' the horns set in beatin' her an' was about to beat her to death an' she told Jack 'f he'd take 'em off she'd give him a pocketbook full of gold. So Jack told 'em to let her alone an' they did.

So hit went on fer a week or two an' the ol' woman didn't pester Jack any more. But one day she come to where he was workin' an' said, "Jack, which do you chose, hard gripes or sharp shins?" He told her hard gripes, an' she jumped on him an' begin chokin' him. He hollered, "Tie, strap, tie, Beat, horns, beat," an' the strap tied her down an' the horns set in beatin' her an' this time they had her nearly beat to death when she started hollerin' fer Jack to take 'em off an' she'd give him a fine hoss, bridle an' saddle. An' he did.

So Jack put on his new suit, put his pocketbook full of gold in his pocket an' got on his hoss an' started out. He was goin' along one day when he seed a lot of people out in a big bottom aroun' a ball set on top of a pole. They had a slick board laid up ag'inst the pole an' a lot of young men was tryin' to ride their hosses up the plank. Jack stopped an' went over an' axed 'em what they was doin'. They told him the King had agreed to give

Polly Johnson. Mrs. Johnson told "Jack and the Bull" (Nos. 3-B and 3-C). Photo courtesy Mrs. Johnson's granddaughter, Estelle Varner.

any man his daughter that would ride his hoss to the top of the pole an' bring back the ball.

Jack axed 'em 'f he could try an' they said yes, hit was free fer all. So Jack he got back on his hoss an' takin' the strap an' horns of his bull in his hands he put the spurs to his hoss an' hollered,

> "Tie, strap, tie,
> Beat, horns, beat."

An' the strap stretched out an' tied aroun' the top of the pole an' the horns hooked his hoss an' he went right on up the plank to the top of the pole an' Jack got the ball an' come down, an' the King's daughter welcomed him at the bottom, an' they married an' was happy.

Collected by James Taylor Adams on October 13, 1941 from Mrs. Polly Johnson of Wise, Virginia. She learned it from her mother.

3-C / *Jack and the Bull*

THERE WAS A BOY BY THE NAME OF JACK. Was a poor boy. He got work herdin' cattle for some folks. They wouldn't feed him. He was about to starve. A strange bull come and jumped into the lot with the cows. Said to Jack, "Jack, I see you're starvin'. You watch till that boy turns his back. Then you beat on my right horn and you'll get bread and cheese, and beat on my left horn and you'll get milk and butter." So Jack watched and eat from the bulls horns, and he was gettin' fat and full. The old woman had two boys. She saw Jack gettin' fat so she sent her two-eyed boy to watch. Jack got his fiddle and played one eye to sleep. Then he played the other eye to sleep. And eat from the bulls horns. The old woman sent her boy with three eyes. Jack played two eyes to sleep, but he couldn't play that last eye to sleep. He got so hongry he went on and knocked on the bull's horns. The boy seed Jack knock on the horns and get bread and cheese and milk and butter. So he told the old woman, and she told her man she wanted that bull's liver and lights. The old man says, "Jack, we'll have to kill that bull." Jack told the bull, and he says, "Now Jack, I'll jump on one of those cows and knock out her liver and lights." So he hooked her and killed her. Jack took the cow's liver and lights to the old man, says, "Here's that old devil bull's liver and lights." The bull told Jack, "Set on my back and we'll leave." So he did, and they travelled on, and travelled on, and travelled on. They went to sleep and the bull dreamed of meetin' another bull. Says, "I'll whip him." They met the bull and Jack's bull whuped him. That night they went to sleep again, and the bull says, "Jack, I dreamed a bad dream. Met a bull with two heads. Finally I whuped him." They went on and heard the bull. Jack hid and watched 'em fight. Jack's bull whuped the other one. They travelled on that day. And next morning Jack's bull says, "Jack, I dreamed a worser dream last night. Met a bull with three heads, and he whuped me this time. We'll meet him today. When you hear that bull you hide. And when he kills me you wait till he goes away, then you skin a strop from the end of my tail plumb up my back and git my horns so you'll git your vittles just the same." So they met that bull with three heads. And they fit and fit, and he killed Jack's bull. So Jack skun a strop from the end of his tail to his horns and got the horns. Jack went on and he was gettin' all raggedy. He come to where there was an old woman. She was a witch. He got him a job. She said, "I'll hire you to herd some sheep." The folks told Jack, "Jack, you'll never see no peace with that old woman. Can't nobody get along with her." Jack says, "I'll stand her off." She come to him, says, "Do you want hard gripes or sharp shins?" He told her he'd take hard gripes. So she went to fight him, and he says, "Tie strop, tie! Beat horns, beat!" So the strop tied the old woman and the horns went to beatin' her, and she hollered. "Let me up and I'll buy you a fine suit of clothes." So Jack let her up. Next day she came right back. Asked him did he want hard gripes or sharp shins. Jack downed her, tied her down and like to beat her to death. "Let me up, Jack, I'll give you a pocket book full of gold and silver." Jack said all right. Next morning she come again, says, "Hard gripes or sharp shins.?" Jack tuk hard gripes and the strop tied her and the horns beat her till she hollered and begged for Jack to let her up and she'd give him a (sure-footed -?-) horse and a bridle and saddle. So Jack tuk his suit of fine clothes and his pocket book and his horse and saddle and bridle, and went on off to seek his fortune. He come to where there was a ball put high up there. And they'd grease a plank and whoever could make a horse go up that plank would get so much money and get the King's daughter. Jack made his horse go up to the plank. And they said "He'll not get that." Jack rode right up and got the ball. Then Jack put on his old raggedy clothes and went to soppin' in the pots. They commenced to beatin' him, says, "Get out of here." Then that ball fell out of his pocket and the King's girl saw it, says, "I know who's got the ball." She told 'em it was Jack. So Jack got on his fine suit of clothes and come in like a fine feller again. And Jack got to marry her.

Collected by Richard Chase on October 13, 1941, from Mrs. Polly Johnson of Wise, Virginia.

3-D / **Jack and His Bull**

ONE TIME THERE WAS A BOY NAMED JACK. His parents were dead and he'd been bound out to a rich man. His job was to feed an' take care of the stock. He'd done somethin' they didn't want him to do an' the old woman wouldn't let him have anything to eat. He was about to starve an' one day when he went to the pasture he was cryin'. He had a bull of his own an' the bull told Jack to screw off his horn an' he'd find food in it. He did that an' was just havin' plenty to eat when the old woman got suspicious. She had three girls, a one-eyed girl, a two-eyed girl and a three-eyed girl. So she sent the one-eyed girl to watch him, but Jack whistled her to sleep and got his somethin' to eat. The next day she sent the two-eyed girl, but Jack whistled her to sleep an' got his somethin' to eat. The next day she sent the three-eyed girl an' Jack whistled two eyes to sleep an' got his

James W. (Little Jim) Hays, Jr., in a photograph from the Bristol Herald Courier, *January, 7, 1951. Mr. Hays told "Jack and His Bull" (No. 3-D). He was also a skilled musician, instrument maker, and wood carver. Here he picks the banjo and makes the little carved figure dance to the tune. Photo courtesy Mr. Hays's granddaughter, Mrs. Virginia Korn.*

somethin' to eat, but the third eye stayed awake an' watched him. She told her mother an' the old woman got to longin' for the bull's melt. Told the old man she just had to have Jack's bull's melt. So they was a-goin' to kill Jack's bull but the bull told Jack to get on his back and they'd go and seek their fortune. So Jack got on his bull an' away they went.

They went on an' on till at last the bull told Jack that they would meet a bear an' they'd have an awful fight, but he'd kill the bear. For Jack to get out of the way while the fight was goin' on. So they did an' Jack clomb a tree an' watched the bull and bear fight. After while the bull killed the bear an' Jack climb down an' got on his bull's back an' they went on their way. They went on an' on till at last the bull told Jack they was goin' to meet a lion an' they'd have an awful fight, but he'd finally kill the lion. So they met up with the old lion and the bull and him fit an' fit an' Jack clomb a tree an' watched 'em. Finally the bull killed the lion an' then Jack climb down outer the tree an' got on his bull's back an' they went on their way. They went on an' on till at last the bull told Jack they was a-goin' to meet up with a tiger. "We'll fight," the bull told him, "an' the tiger will finally kill me. When it does," the bull said, "you skin a strip off of my back from end of my tail to tip of my nose an' take it with you an' anything you want tied it will tie." So they went on an' met the old tiger an' him and the bull fit and fit an' finally the tiger killed Jack's bull. Jack waited till the tiger had gone off an' then he climb down from the tree an' skun a strip from the end of his bull's tail to the tip of his nose an' went on his way.

Jack went on an' on till he come to a big apple orchard. He was hungry an' was goin' to git some apples when the farmer come a-runnin' an' told him to stay out of his orchard. Jack throwed down his strip from his bull's back an' says, "Tie him up." An' the strip tied him up han' an' foot an' Jack got all the apples he wanted, then untied the farmer an' took his strip from the bull's back an' went on to seek his fortune.

Collected by James Taylor Adams on January 21, 1942, from James W. (Little Jim) Hays, Jr., of St. Paul, Virginia. He heard his father tell it.

3-E / *Jack and His Bull*

ONE TIME THEY WAS AN OLD MAN and an old woman that had took a boy to raise. The boy's name was Jack. The old man liked Jack and had give him a bull calf to raise for his own. The old woman hated Jack and she tried to keep her old man from giving Jack the calf but he wouldn't listen to her. He give Jack the calf anyway.

Well hit went on till the calf was grown. A big fine blue bull. The old woman hated Jack more and more. She decided to starve Jack's bull to death. She told the boys not to give Jack's bull a bite and to mind him off from where the other cattle was eating. They did, an' Jack's bull was getting poor as a snake.

So Jack he got to setting up of a night and slipping out about midnight and feeding his bull. And the bull was gitting jest as fat as a pig. So the old woman she noticed Jack's bull was getting fat and she told the old man she was in a family way and was longing fer Jack's bull's melt. The old man didn't want to kill the bull, but she kept right on and on, tell finally he agreed to

23

kill him and give Jack another calf. He told Jack what he was going to do. Now Jack he thought a lot of his blue bull and that night when he went to feed him he told him they was going to kill him. "Well, Jack," said the bull, "me and you had better get away from here. You just hop up on my back and we will go."

Jack hopped up on his blue bull's back and away they went. By daylight they were away out of the country. They went on and on and met up with a big white bull. Him and Jack's bull had a fight and Jack's bull killed him. And they went on and on and met up with a big red bull. Him and Jack's bull had a fight and Jack's bull finally killed the red bull. They then went on and they heard another bull bellowing on ahead. Jack's bull told him that that was a big black bull and that he would be bigger than any of the rest and that he would be killed by this big black bull and for Jack to saw off one of his horns after he was dead and anytime he was in trouble or needed anything just blow the horn and he'd get it. So they went on and met the big black bull and him and Jack's blue bull had an awful fight and at last the big black bull killed Jack's bull. Jack cried, but he done what his bull told him to do: he sawed one of his horns and went on.

One day he come to where some young men was trying to climb a slick pole that had five dollars on it. None of them could get to the top. So Jack he blowed his bull's horn and tried to climb it and he just went right on up and got the five dollars. Then they told him the King's daughter was chosing her husband. He went in and she wouldn't speak to him because his clothes were not good. He stepped behind the house and blowed his bull's horn and he had a fine suit on and went back in and she chose him and they married and when the King died Jack was the King and the last time I heard from him he was gettin' along just fine.

Collected by James Taylor Adams on November 24, 1941, from James Pilkenton, 13-year-old son of Orville Pilkenton of Pound, Virginia. James heard the tale from his grandmother Pilkenton.

4 / *Jack and His Lump of Silver*

JACK WHO HAD BEEN A GOOD WORKER for his master in England for several years grew tired and lazy but his master told him he had been a good worker and would pay him well. He gave him a big lump of silver as big as his head. Jack started on his trip to his home to see his father and mother but grew very tired on the way as the silver grew heavier. Soon he sat down to rest when a man on a pretty horse rode by in a swirl of dust. He sat upright and held his head high. Jack stopped the man and told him it was a pretty and good horse and it seemed easy enough to ride. The man finally talked him into a swap for the silver in return for the horse and told Jack when he wanted to ride fast to say, "Git up." Jack got on and rode off. Later he thought he would like to ride fast and said to the horse," Git up," and the horse bolted from under him and he fell into the road in the dirt. As he got up he saw a man coming up the road driving a cow and told him he would swap the horse for the cow which he did. Later he grew hungry and wanted some milk to eat with his bread he had brought along and he tried to milk the cow but she kicked him and jumped to one side. At that time a man came along with a pig tied by the hind leg and laughed at him trying to milk the cow. Jack was worried and said that he could eat the pig meat and would swap with the man. The man as usual was eager for the trade and made off down the road with his cow and Jack went the other way with his pig. But the pig wanted to go in the opposite direction and Jack couldn't do anything with it and didn't know what he was going to do about his position. But luck was with him he thought as he saw a man coming with a white goose under his arm. He swapped the pig for the goose and went off down the road in lighter spirits. The goose could lay an egg and he wouldn't go hungry and he could sell the feathers, he thought. As he neared a small town he met a man with a grind stone grinding away and a whistle on his lips as he ground. "I whistle because I always find money in my pocket all the time. It is a

25

Amy Fuller Vicars. Mrs. Vicars told "Jack and His Lump of Silver" (No. 4). Photo courtesy Mrs. Vicars's grand-daugher, Mrs. Amy Dean Wills.

good grinder that can do that." Jack thought it was too and he told the man he would trade the grindstone for the goose if he wished and this he did. He went down the road happy with the stone on his back. But later he grew tired and the stone heavy and he grew thirsty too. He spied a well and looked into it to see if he could see water. As he did so the stone fell into the well with a loud noise. "Oh well," thought Jack, "I have nothing to worry me now and nothing to carry and make me tired," so he sat down on the side of the road and ate the dry bread happily that he had nothing to worry him more.

Collected by James M. Hylton on November 17, 1941, from Mrs. A.M. (Amy) Vicars, aged 79 years. Her mother, Aunt Cynthia Jessee Fuller, told her many tales brought over from England and Scotland. Mrs. Vicars does not recall how long it has been since she heard this tale. She said that the young children of her day and time knew no other tales but the ones brought over by early settlers from England and other countries. Type 1415, "Lucky Hans."

5 / *Jack and Mossyfoot*

ONE TIME THERE WAS A WOMAN who was a widow and she had one boy named Jack. Jack disobeyed his mother one day and she whipped him. He decided he was going to run away. He went down the road and lay down under a tree and after while he got up and went down the road and by night he was away off in the woods. He was sort of afraid out there by hisself and built him a fire to keep him company. After awhile he heard something coming, "Whoomity whop, whoomity whop." He looked and there came the awfulest thing he had ever seen in his life. Oh it had eyes as big as saucers and like balls of fire and its legs were ten feet long, its tail fifteen feet long, and its feet were long and covered with moss. So Jack knowed right off it was a mossyfoot. He was scared. He grabbed up a chunk and throwed it at the mossyfoot and it went off. But soon he heard it coming again, "Whoomity whop, whoomity whop." And its eyes like big balls of fire. He throwed another firey chunk at it and it ran off again. But soon hit was back again, "Whoomity whop, whoomity whop," and its eyes shining like balls of fire. He throwed his last chunk at it. It ran off, but soon he saw hit's big eyes shining and heard hit coming, "Whoomity whop, whoomity whop." He ran this time and clomb a tall hickory. But right on it come, "Whoomity whop, whoomity whop," and its eye shining like balls of fire. Hit began to gnaw at the roots of the tree, just "gnawity gnaw, gnawity gnaw." And hit wasn't long till the tree began to fall. Jack thought he was a goner as the tree came down and down, but just before hit struck the ground he woke up.

Collected by James Taylor Adams on February 5, 1942, at the Flat Gap High School from Glady Bolling, 17-year-old daughter of Henderson Bolling. Glady learned it from Shelby Bolling and he, in turn, from Boyd Bolling.

6-A / Jack and Old King Morock

ONE TIME THERE WAS A BOY named Jack and he left home and went off to seek his fortune. He got to gambling and one day he met up with King Morock and they started gambling. Now old King Morock was a witch, but Jack didn't know hit. They agreed that if King Morock beat Jack that he'd cut off Jack's head and if Jack beat him he could have his choice of King Morock's three daughters for a wife.

So they played and Jack won. Then King Morock he cast a spell over Jack and disappeared. Jack didn't know which way he went and he didn't know a thing about where he lived. But he meant to find him and claim his daughter so he started out asking everybody he come across if they knowed where King Morock lived. Nobody knowed, but at last he met up with a man named Frostwell and he asked him if he knowed where King Morock lived. He said no, but that he would frost the earth and see if he could frost him out. So he frosted the earth, but he couldn't find King Morock. So Jack went on. At last he met up with a man named Freezewell and he asked him if he knew where King Morock lived. He said no, but he would freeze the earth and see if he could freeze him out. So he froze the whole earth, but King Morock didn't come out. Then Freezewell told Jack that he knew an old man who kept beer to sell that could tell him where King Morock's three daughters washed. "But," he said, "this old man is mad at me for freezin' up his beer an' you'll have to make up with him. I'll give you a rod and you take hit and hit will thaw out his beer and he'll be in good humor and will tell you where King Morock's daughters go to wash."

So Jack went the way that Freezewell told him to go and he come to the old man's house. He went in and told him he wanted to buy a drink of beer. He said he'd be glad to sell hit to him, but Freezewell had hit all froze up and he couldn't get hit out. Jack told him he'd thaw hit up for him if he'd tell him where the three daughters of old King Morock went to wash. He said all right, an' Jack took his rod and passed it about the place

28

and everything thawed up an' he poured Jack out some beer and told him to go to a certain place and hide himself on the bank of the river and he'd see the daughters of King Morock when they come to wash.

So Jack he went on like the old beer seller told him to go and hid under a big log. Didn't have to wait long. Just about the time the sun was rising he looked up and there come the prettiest girl he'd ever seen out of the woods with a greyhound skin around her. She pulled hit off and throwed hit up on the log that Jack was hid under, but out of his reach. Then she waded out in the river and washed. After she got herself washed she waded out and reached up and got her greyhound skin and put hit on and went back in the woods. She hadn't been gone but a little while till Jack looked up an' here come another girl. She pulled off her greyhound skin and tossed hit on the log out of Jack's reach. Then she waded out in the water and washed herself. Oh, she was prettier than the other one. She was the prettiest girl Jack had ever seed in all his life. After she had washed she come out an' reached up an' got her greyhound skin and put hit on an' went back in the woods. She hadn't been gone but a little while till Jack looked up and seed another girl a-coming. She come on an' pulled off her greyhound skin an' tossed it up on the log, but hit slid off right by Jack an' she didn't notice it. So she went on in the water and washed herself, an' Jack knowed she was the prettiest girl he'd ever seed in all his life. She was a lot prettier than the last one. So she finished washin' herself and come out to get her greyhound skin, but Jack had it an' wouldn't give hit to her unless she'd take him to King Morock's house. She said she couldn't do that. Her father would kill her if she did. He said if she didn't take him to her father's house she couldn't have her greyhound skin. She said she wouldn't take him to the house, but if he'd promise to do what she told him that she'd take him to the gate. He promised he would and he give her her greyhound skin and they went on together. They got to the gate an' she told him to wait right there till daylight the next morning and then he could come on in, and that when King Morock saw him he'd put him to cleaning out a stable that hadn't been cleaned out in seven years and a gold ring was lost in it and hit would have to be found. "He'll bring you two shevels," she said, "an old shevel and a new one. You take the old one." Jack promised her he'd do what she'd told him and she went on in and left him at the gate.

So Jack stayed at the gate all that night and bright and early he went in and King Morock met him at the door. "Hah," said King Morock, "I see you've found me, Jack. Some of my people must have been working against me." Jack told him no, that he'd just kept on hunting an' sarchin' till he found where he lived. "Well," said old King Morock, "I'm pretty glad you've come, Jack. I've got some work I want you to do. Come on in and get your breakfast!"

So Jack he went in and eat a hearty breakfast and after breakfast old King Morock he took Jack out to the stable and told him the stable hadn't been cleaned out in seven years and he wanted him to clean out and find a gold ring that had been lost in it. He brought out two shevels: a new shevel and one so old that hit was all rusted and the handle just hanging to it. He told Jack to take his pick an' Jack he studied a minute and took the new one and started in shevelin' the manure out of the stable. But ever time he'd throw out one shevelfull two would be sheveled in. So hit wasn't but a little while till the stable was full of manure, and Jack, knowing his life was in parrell [peril], sot down on the doorsill and put his head in his hands and started crying. He heard somebody comin' an' he looked up an' seed the youngest daughter of old King Morock a-comin'. She come on up an' said, "What are you cryin' about, Jack?" He showed her the stable plum full of manure and told her what had happened. "Well," she said, "Didn't I tell you to chose the old shevel?" Jack said yes, but hit was so awful old that he couldn't have done anything with it. Then she pulled the old shevel out from under [her] aporn an' just sheveled out one shevelfull of manure and all the rest followed it, and the stable was just as clean as your hand and there laid the ring. She then told Jack not to go back to the house till next mornin' and then take the ring and go in. She said that her father would send him to ketch a mare that hadn't been ketched in seven years, and that he'd let him choose between an old and a new bridle and for him to take the old bridle. Jack promised her he'd do what she told him.

So Jack he stayed at the stable all night and bright and early the next morning he went to the house and old King Morock met him at the door. "Hah," said the old King Morock, "I see you found my ring, Jack. Surely some of my people have been working against me." But Jack told him no, that he was a good hardworkin' boy and that he had been a time at hit, but he finally got the manure all sheveled out of the stable and found the ring. King Morock then told Jack to come on in and eat his breakfast that he had another job for him. So Jack went in and eat his breakfast and after breakfast King Morock called him out in the yard and told him that he had a mare that hadn't been ketched in seven years and he wanted him to go over in the woodland pasture and ketch her and bring her in. And he brought out two bridles: a brandnew bridle and an old, old bridle that was just barely hanging together. "Chose quick," he told Jack. "Your life's in parrel if you don't ketch the mare." And Jack he studied a minute and took the new bridle.

So Jack he went over in the pasture and found the mare. She seed Jack a-comin' and she tossed up her tail, throwed up her head, snorted and whinnied and took down the hill and across the valley with Jack right after her. She would run up one hill and when Jack got there she'd be going down the hill and back across the valley to the other. So Jack just run and run and run till he was plum give out an' he sot down on a log and put his head in his hands and started crying. He heard somebody a walkin' and looked up and there come the girl. "What's the matter, Jack?" she axed him. He told her about the mare and that he couldn't ketch her. "Well," she said, "Why didn't you chose the old bridle like I told you to?" "Oh," said Jack, "Hit was old, hit wouldn't hold anything." She pulled the old bridle out from under her aporn and held hit up and the mare just come a trottin' and put her head right in it. "Now," said the girl, "You stay out here till daylight in the mornin' and then take the mare an' go in. My father will have another job for you. He'll tell you to build a boat and sail across the Red Sea and climb a long slick sycamore tree to the very top and bring him three crow's eggs back. Now you can't do that, but I can. I'll do hit for you. You go down to the beach and I'll meet you there and help you."

So Jack he stayed out in the pasture all night and about daylight the next morning he went to the house leading the mare. Old King Morock come out and met him. "Hah," he said, "I see you've ketched my mare, Jack. Surely some of my people have been working against me." Jack told him no, that he had a time of it ketching the mare, but that he was a fast runner and he'd finally run her down and bridled her. King Morock then told Jack to come on in and eat his breakfast and that he had another job for him. So Jack went in and eat a hearty breakfast and after breakfast King Morock called him out and told him that there was a crow's nest in the topmost bough of a long slick sycamore that stood on the other side of the Red Sea and that he wanted Jack to go across the Red Sea and climb that long slick sycamore tree and bring him three eggs out of the crow's nest.

So Jack he told King Morock that was quite a job, but he'd do his best. And old King Morock told him he'd better not fail for if he did his life would be in parrel. Then Jack he went down to the beach and sot down on a big flat rock to wait for the girl to come. He sot there and sot there. The day was over half gone and he'd give her out a-comin' and he put his head in his hands and started cryin'. Then he heard somebody a-coming walking and he looked up and seed her a-coming a-running torge him. She come on up and said, "What are you cryin' about, Jack?" "Oh," said Jack, "I'd give you out a-comin' an' I didn't know what in the world to do." She told him to hush and she knocked her up a ship and sailed off across the Red Sea and when she got to the long slick sycamore her finger nails turned to claws and her toe nails turned to spikes and she just clum right on up the long slick sycamore and got the crow's eggs and brought them back and give them to Jack. "Now," the girl said to Jack, "you stay here till in the morning and then you take the crow's eggs and go and give them to my father, and he'll tell you that the time has come for you to chose one of his daughters for your wife. Which one will you chose?" "I'll chose you of course," Jack told her. "Well," she said, "We will all look exactly alike and how are you going to know me from my sisters?" Jack didn't know that. But she told him that for him to keep his eyes on their faces and she would lick out her tongue at him.

So Jack he stayed there on the bank of the Red Sea till daylight the next morning and then he took the three crow's eggs and went to King Morock's with them. "Hah," said old King Morock, "I see you got the crow's eggs, Jack. Surely some of my people have been working against me." But Jack told him no, that he had allus been a good boatman and a good climber and hit was a pretty good job but he finally got the eggs. King Morock then told Jack to come on in and eat his breakfast and that after breakfast he had something else for him to do.

So Jack he went on in and eat a hearty breakfast and after breakfast King Morock called him out in the yard and told him the time had come when he would chose one of his daughters for a wife. There they stood side by side dressed in their greyhound skins and to save his life Jack couldn't tell one of them from the other. King Morock said, "You have just one minute to make your choice. If you don't make your choice in that time I'm going to cut your head off. So Jack he kept looking straight at the girls' faces and he seed the middle one lick out her tongue at him. He told King Morock that he'd take the middle girl. King Morock told him all right, but she was his youngest and prettiest girl.

Jack and the girl went in a room and went to bed together and way long in the night Jack waked up and the girl was a-crying and a-snubbin'. He axed her what was the matter and she told him that her father had made her promise to kill him before daylight. "Well," axed Jack, "What are we goin' to do?" She said, "les slip out an' run away." "All right," said Jack. And they slipped out of the house and went to the stable and the girl got the old, old bridle and they went to the woodland pasture and she just held it up and here come the mare and put her head in it and took the bits in her mouth and they got on her and away they went.

They rid on and on till hit come daylight and the girl said to Jack, "Feel under the mare's right ear an' see what you feel." Jack did and said, "I feel bad roads, logs and rocks." The girl said, "Wish hit all behind you and a clear road ahead of you." And Jack did and all at once all behind them was rough roads filled with rocks and crossed by logs, and old King Morock and his men who had discovered that they'd run away was following them, come to the rocks and logs and they had to turn around and go back to git something to clean them out with and Jack and the girl got another good start on 'em.

So they rid on and on till late in the evening when the girl said to Jack, "Feel under the mare's left ear and see what you feel." Jack did and said, "I feel bad roads and high water." The girl said, "Wish hit all behind you and a clear road before you." And Jack did and all at once there was great floods and a sea of water all over the road they had just passed. Old King Morock come to the water and couldn't git across and he just give up and went back home.

Jack had been away from home a long time and he decided to go and see his folks. The girl said she'd not go in, but would wait at the gate for him. She told him not to let anything touch his lips while he was away from her and if he did he would forget her. He told her he wouldn't and left her at the gate and went on in. All of his folks come a-runnin' to meet him and threw their arms around him and tried to kiss him, but he held his hand over his mouth to keep them from touching his lips. So he went on in and he'd had a little dog before he left that was a great fool about him. Hit come running to where he was settin' and jumped up in his lap and before he could stop hit hit had kissed him on the lips. He forgot the girl right then and settled down at home as he had been before he started off to seek his fortune.

The girl she waited at the gate all that day and that night, but next morning she knew he had let something touch his lips and had forgotten her, so she started out by herself. She was tired and hungry and she come to a spring with a stooping tree standing over it. She drunk and then crawled up in the tree to rest. Now there was an old shoemaker lived near there and he had a wife and one daughter and all three of them were very homely and ugly. They packed water from that spring, and that day the girl went to the spring to get a bucket of water. She stooped over to dip up the water and seed the girl's reflection in the spring. She thought hit was herself she seed and she said, "Oh, if I'm that pretty I'm a fool for stayin' with two ugly old people like my father and mother. I'll just leave and some fine young man will chose me for his wife." So she went off through the woods. Wasn't long till the old woman come to see what was a keepin' the girl and she seed the girl's reflection in the spring and she thought hit was herself and she said, "Humph! If I'm that pretty I'm a fool to live with an old ugly man like I've got. I'll just leave him and some fine rich man will take me for his wife." And she went off through the woods too.

So the old man he got oneasy about his wife and daughter and went to see what was a keeping them. He got to the spring and looked in the water and seed the girl's reflection. He knew he wasn't that good looking and he got to looking about and saw her up in the tree. He asked her what she was doing there and she told him what had happened to her, but didn't tell him who her husband was. He axed her how she would like to hire to him to do his work now that his wife and daughter had left him. She said all right and she got down and went to the house with him.

Now Jack he had had a sweetheart before he went off to seek his fortune and he went to see her again and they set the day to be married. Nearly everybody was going to the wedding. So one day a young man in the neighborhood went to the old shoemaker to get him a pair of new shoes made to wear to Jack's wedding. Hit took all day and part of the night to make the new shoes so he had to stay all night there. He seed the girl and thought she was awful pretty and he axed how about sleeping with her that night. She said all right. So they went in to go to bed and she said, "I don't want to crawl to bed to a man, you let me get in first." So he said all right and she got in and he had just pulled off when all at once she said, "I had a calf to tie up and forgot it. Will you go out and tie hit up for me?" So the young man went out to tie hit up and got the rope around hit's neck and she said, "Have you got hit roped?" He said yes. "Well," she said, "You hold hit and hit hold you till mornin'." And he had to stand there holding the calf all night in his shirt tail. And next morning he gave her ten dollars not to tell hit on him.

The next day another young man come to get a pair of shoes made and he had to stay all night. He seed the girl and got struck on her and he axed her how about sleeping with her that night. She said all right. When they went in to go to bed she said, "I don't want to crawl to bed to a man, you let me get in first." So he said all right and she got in and he had just pulled off when she said, "Oh, I had a gander to pen. Will you pen him for me?" He said yes and he went out in his shirt tail and grabbed the old gander and he started beating him with his wings. She hollered out to him, "Have you got a hold of him?" He said yes and she said, "All right, you hold him and he'll hold you till morning." And he stayed there all night fighting with the old gander. The next morning he gave her ten dollars not to tell hit on him.

The next day Jack come to have his wedding boots made. He had to stay all night. He seed the girl and he just went crazy about her. He axed her how about sleeping with her that night and she said all right. So they went in the room and she said, "I don't want to crawl to bed to a man, so you let me get in first." He said all right. So she got in the bed and he had just pulled off when she said, "Oh, I forgot to kiver up the fire. Will you kiver hit up for me?" He said yes and kivered up the fire when she said, "Have you got hit kivered up?" He said yes and she said, "All right just set there and pity-to-pat hit till morning." So he set there and pity-to-patted the fire till morning. And he give her ten dollars not to tell hit on him.

The next day was Jack's wedding day. The shoemaker was goin' and he axed the girl if she wanted to go. She said no, but after he'd gone she went on after him. Jack and his girl was just standin' up when she walked up in the yard. She pulled a little

Nancy (Old Granny) Shores on the Mullins Fork of Bold Camp, Wise County. Mrs. Shores was a midwife and caught an estimated one thousand babies in her lifetime. She told James Taylor Adams the tale of "Jack and Old King Morock" (No. 6-A). Photo from Luther F. Addington, The Story of Wise County (Virginia), and used with permission of Mrs. Luther F. Addington.

box out of her pocket and out jumped a hen and rooster. Then she reached in the other pocket and got some barley and throwed hit on the ground. The hen begun pecking at the barley and the rooster begun pecking at her. The girl says, "Hold on there my fine feller, I guess you forget the time I saved your head by cleaning out a stable for you and finding a gold ring." Jack heard her and something seemed to come over him. She took out another handful of barley and throwed it to the chickens and the hen started pecking at the barley and the rooster started pecking at her. The girl says, "Hold on there my fine feller, I guess you forget the time I saved your head by ketching a mare that hadn't been ketched in seven years." By this time Jack had left his bride's side and stepped to the door. The girl throwed some more barley on the ground and the hen started pecking at the barley and the rooster started pecking at her. The girl says, "Hold on there my fine feller, I guess you forget the time I saved your head by sailing the Red Sea and climbing a long slick sycamore tree and getting three crow's eggs for old King Morock's pleasure."

Then hit all come back to Jack. He remembered her. And he made his apologies to the other girl and the people and they went away together and the last time I heard from them they were living happy.

Collected by James Taylor Adams on February 12, 1942, from Nancy (Old Granny) Shores on the Mullins Fork of Bold Camp, Wise County, Virginia. Type 313, "The Girl as Helper in the Hero's Flight." See Chase, Jack Tales, JACK AND KING MOROCK. *For an Afro-American version of this tale see, Richard Dorson,* American Negro Folktales *(Greenwich, CT: Fawcett Publications, Inc., 1967) 268-271.*

6-B / *Willie and the Devil*

I GUESS IT IS SO. Pa used to tell hit to us youngins.

Said thar'uz a young man an' his name was Willie. He had one brother an' he'd married an' moved way off sumers. He didn't know jes 'zactly where he did live.

Willie'uz an awful gambler. Ever'body he met he tackle 'em for a poker game.

One day he'uz out runnin' 'round an' met the Devil. He didn't know he'uz the Devil. So he tackled 'im for a poker game. So they started in playin'. The Devil had a whole gallon of gold an' in jes a little while Willie had won it.

The Devil was mad 'cause he'd lost all o' his gold, an' he told Willie, he says, "You come to my house next Saturday night an' we'll play some more, an' 'f ye don't I'll kill ye an' put yo' head on a spear."

Willie was in a quandry. He didn't know hardly what to do. He know'd the Devil would keep 'is word an' kill 'im 'f he didn't go to his house an' he didn't know how to git thar. At last on Wednesday he made up his mind to start out an' see 'f he could find the Devil's house. An' he did. He started out goin' west. He traveled all that day hoping to find his brother's house an' about sundown he did. He stayed all night with his brother an' his brother noticed he was in trouble an' he axed him, he says, "What's the matter Willie? What makes ye ack this a way?" An' Wilie tol' 'im he had to find the Devil's house by Saturday night or the Devil would kill 'im an' put his head on the end of a spear. His brother hooted at him. He says, "Ah, Willie, you acktin' the fool. The Devil won't bother ye 'f ye'll go about yo' own business." But Willie was afraid he would an' he got up bright an' early next mornin' and struck out.

So he went on an' on. Traveled all that day an' the next an' hit was gittin' late Saturday an' he hadn't seed a livin' soul since he left his brother's Thursday mornin'. He had had nothin' to eat 'sept jes what few berries an' things he picked in the woods as he went along, an' he'uz nearly starved to death. He'uz goin' long an' over to one side of him was a big river. All at once he heard a splashin' over thar an' somebody hollerin' an' goin' on an' laughin'. He looked hard an' seed three pritty girls in a swimmin'. He decided he'd go over an' watch 'em swim awhile. Didn't look like he'uz goin' to find the Devil's house nohow.

So he went over an' sot down on the bank an' watched the girls swim. At last they seed 'im an' they all come swimmin' to the bank an' crawled out an' sot down by 'im. They'uz one of them the prittiest girl he'd ever seed in all his life.

They bagged 'im to come in an' swim with 'em. An' he tol' 'em he couldn't swim. The prittiest one of 'em took out a gold needle an' told 'im to stick hit in his coat an' he did an' there he stood in a bathin' suit an' he went in an' could swim like a duck. After they'd swum awhile they all got out an' two of the girls jes riz an' flew off like birds across the mountains. The other girl, the pritty one, said to him, "'F ye want to go with me ye can fly, too." He tol' her he was lookin' for the Devil an' had to find him by dark. She laughed and told him, she says, "We're the Devil's daughters. 'F ye will go with me I'll take you right smack to 'im." So she give 'im a gold pin an' he stuck hit in his coat. All at once he had wings, jes growed on his side right thar, an' they riz up an' flew off side by side across the mountains. They flew an' they flew an' at last the girl said to him, says she, "When we git thar ye'd better light before we git to the house an' walk in." So he lit when they got in sight of the Devil's house an' she flew on an' lit in the yard. He walked on up an' knocked on the door an' out come the ol' Devil. "Oh, hit's you, is it?" He invited him in an' that night after supper they went into a room an' locked the door an' the Devil had a whole peck o' gold. An' they started playin' poker, an' they played for about an' hour an' Willie won hit ever' bit.

Next mornin' they got up an' after breakfast the Devil called Willie out an' told 'im, he says, "My great-grandmother lost her gold ring down thar in that stable. You find hit by the time I git home tonight an' we'll play some more poker. An' 'f ye don't I'll kill ye an' stick yo head on the end of a spear. I've got to go out in the worl' an' look after my business today." An' he was off an' gone.

So Willie got 'im a pick an' a shevel an' went down to the stable an' started diggin' in the manure. Thar wudn't more'n six inches of manure when he started but by noon the stable was full an' hit was runnin' out at the cracks. The more he dug an' sheveled, the more thar wuz. At twelve the pritty girl come out an' hollered, "Come on to dinner, Willie." "No, I can't come now," he told her, "I've got to find that ring or the Devil will cut off my head an' stick hit on the end of a spear." She tol' him to come on an' eat an' she'd go back an' help 'im after dinner. So he drapped his tools an' went on to the house an' eat his dinner.

After dinner she went down to the stable with 'im. The manure was runnin' out at ever' crack an' crivice. She handed him a little gold shevel she took out o' her bosom an' told him to shevel with hit. He sheveled three shevel fulls an' low an' behold the manure was all gone an' the floor'uz jes as clean as yo han' an' thar, right in the middle of the floor layed the ring. So he got hit an' that night when the Devil come in he said, "Well, Willie, did ye find my great-grandmother's ring?" Willie tol' 'im yes an' took hit out an' give hit to him. He looked at Willie sorty funny, but didn't say nothin'.

Well, that night after supper, the Devil took Willie in a room an' he had a whole half a bushel of gold. So they sot in to playin' poker an' they played a right smart bit an' Willie won hit ever' bit.

The next mornin' they got up an' after breakfast the Devil called Willie out an' told him, he says, "My great-great-grandmother lost her thimble in that well. Ye draw out the water an' find hit by the time I come back tonight an' we'll play some more poker, an' 'f ye don't I'll cut off yo head an' stick hit on the end of a spear. An' the Devil went off.

Willie got him a bucket an' a rope an' went out to the well an' looked down in it. Didn't seem to be more'n two or three gallons of water in it, but when he started drawin' hit started rizin' an' by noon the water was runnin' out of the top of the well. Oh, the sweat was jes a pourin' off of Willie. He couldn't gain a bit on hit. The pritty girl come out an' hollered, "Come on to dinner, Willie." "Oh, I can't come now," he told her, "I've got to git this water out of the well an' find the Devil's great-great-grand-mother's thimble or he'll cut off my head an' stick hit on the end of a spear." She told him to come on an' eat an' she'd go back with 'im an' help him after dinner. So he went on an' eat.

After dinner she went back with 'im an' handed 'im a little gold cup she'd took out of her bosom an' told 'im to dip out three cup fulls. He did an' the well was dry. Wudn't no sign of water anywhere, an' he looked down in the well an' thar laid the thimble. He got hit an' that night when the Devil come in he said, "Oh, Willie, did ye find my great-great-grandmother's thimble?" An' Willie handed hit to him.

That night after supper they went in the room an' locked the door an' the Devil had a whole bushel of gold. They started in to play poker an' they played and they played and they played. Played tell 'bout midnight an' Willie finally won hit all.

Next mornin' they got up an' after breakfast the Devil called Willie out an' got a big hammer an' chisel an' took 'im down on the side of the hill where thar's a great ol' big rock. He told Willie, he says, "I'm goin' off on my business today. I'll be back tonight. I want you to set in an' build me a house twelve stories high with twelve rooms, twelve feet square, on each story. Build hit out 'o this rock. 'F ye have it done an' ready for me to move in when I git back tonight we'll play some more poker an' 'f ye don't I'll cut off yo head an' stick it on the end of a spear."

Well, that'uz an awful lookin' job for one day, but Willie decided thar's nothin' to do but try an' see what heppened. So he set in on the rock. An' he pounded an' he chiseled an' the more he broke off the rock the bigger it got. At twelve the pritty girl come out and hollered, "Come on to dinner, Willie." "Oh, no, I jes can't come this time. I hain't got nothin' done an' I must have a house twelve stories high with twelve rooms, twelve feet square on each story built by the time the Devil gits back or he'll cut off my head and stick it on the end of a spear." She told him to come on an' eat an' after dinner she'd go back an' help him. So he decided she had helped 'im an' that he'd go an' eat an' see what happened. So he did an' after dinner she went back with him. She reached in her bosom an' took out a little gold hammer an' a little gold chisel an' give 'em to 'im an' told 'im to strike three licks. He did an' she said, "Now look behind ye!" He looked an' thar was a stone house twelve stories high, with twelve rooms, twelve feet square on ever' floor. An' they went all through hit an' hit was all fixed up an' finished jes ready to live in.

"Now," she told Willie, "when you see the Devil a-comin' you go out an' meet him 'fore he gits here. Take 'im all through the house an' he'll be pleased with hit. Then as he comes on to the house he'll be studyin' about hit an' will turn an' look back at it. An' hit'll not be thar. He will start in ravin' at you about hit bein' gone an' you tell him you contracted to build hit, not to make hit stay thar."

So he did. That evenin' he looked out an' seed the Devil a-comin'. He went out an' met him. "Well, well, well, Willie," he said, "I see you built my house. How did you do hit?" An' he looked at Willie as though he expected sumpin'. Willie tol' 'im to come on an' they went all through hit an' the Devil was awful well pleased with hit. Then as they was goin' to the house he turned to look back an' hit wasn't thar. Jes the big rock like hit was that mornin' when Willie started in on it. "Where's my house?" the Devil looked at Willie like he'd jump through him. "I contracted to build hit an' not to make hit stay thar," Willie answered him back. The Devil was awful mad, but he didn't say nothin' more. But he was afraid of Willie an' wouldn't play no more poker with 'im. An' next mornin' when the Devil left he didn't leave Willie anything to do.

After the Devil had left the pritty girl tol' Willie, she said, "You go out to the stable an' catch the poorest mule an' poorest hoss you can fin' an' bring 'em out here an' we'll run away an' git married." So Willie done what she told 'im to do. An' they'uz jes skin an' bones. He hitched 'em up in front of the house an' she come out an' told 'im to git her a saddle for the mule an' he went an' got one an' rech it to her an' she throwed hit on the mule an' all at once hit 'uz the finest an' fatest mule he'd ever seed. As slick as a ribbon. She tol' him to reach 'er another saddle an' he rech her another an' she throwed hit on the ol' poor hoss an' he wuz jes as fat as his hide could hol' 'im an' slick as could be.

They got up an' rid off. She tol' him the Devil'ud foller 'em when 'e found hit out an' for him to keep a watch out behin'.

They went on an' on an' at last on a long stretch of road Willie looked back an' seed the Devil a-comin' jes a tearin' after 'em. She said you git down an' dip up a thimblefull of water an' pour in my mule's year. An he did an' all at once all between them an' the Devil'uz jes one big river an' the Devil had to go back an' git a gold cup and dip hit dry an' by that time they'd gained a right smart on 'im.

So they went on an' on an' on. Then Willie looked back ag'in an' seed the Devil a-comin' jes tearin' behin' 'em.
The girl told 'im to git down an' git a thorn an' stick in her mule's year. He did an' all at once all between them an' the Devil was jes one big thorn thicket. A rabbit couldn't got through it. So the Devil had to stop an' turn roun' an' go back home an' git a gold axe to cut a way through the thorns an' by that time they'd got a pritty good gain on 'im.

So they went on an' on an' on. Then Willie looked back ag'in an' seed the Devil jes a rarin' an' tearin' behin' 'em. The girl tol' him to git down off 'is hoss an' git a gravel an' put in her mule's year. An' Willie did an' low an' behol' all the country between them an' the Devil was jes one big rock piled on top of another. An' the Devil had to stop an' turn 'roun' an' go back an' git a gold hammer to break 'im a way through 'em. An' before he got the rocks out an' ketched up with 'em ga'in they'd got to the settlements an' got married an' lived a happy life forever after.

Collected by James Taylor Adams on July 8, 1941, from Gaines Kilgore, Birchfield Creek, Wise County, Virginia. He heard his father tell it about 1915.

6-C / *Willie and the Devil*

ONE TIME THEY WAS A YOUNG FELLER named Willie. He was a pretty rowdy sort of boy an' he got to gamblin'. Got so that he'd banter ever'body he met for a game of cards. Preachers or jis anybody.

One day he was goin' 'long when he met up with the Devil. So he tackled him for a game of cards. They sot down an' went to playin'. The Devil beat Willie seven straight games. Willie then turned it on him and beat him seven. The Devil didn't like it, so he told Willie that he'd have to be at his house by the next Saturday night shore or his head would be cut off an' put on a spear.

Willie believed the Devil and thought he'd have to go to the Devil's house, but he didn't know where he lived an' the Devil hadn't told him how to git thar.

Well he started out on Monday mornin'. He traveled all week, up till Friday evenin' askin' ever'body he met if they knowed where the Devil lived an' none of 'em could tell him. Friday night he got to his brother's. His brother had married and moved away off there. He stayed all night with his brother an' his brother noticed he was in trouble some way. So next mornin' he axed him what was the matter, an' Willie told him that he was goin' to the Devil an' axed him if he knowed where he stayed. His brother knowed nothin' about the Devil, an' he tried to persuade Willie to give up the journey an' stay with him, but Willie said no he had to go or his head would be on the spear shore.

So Willie hit out early Saturday mornin' an' about twelve that day as he was goin' along he looked down under the bank an' seed two girls a-swimmin' in the river. So he thought they might know sump'n about the Devil an' he went down an' hollered an' axed 'em. One of them was awful pretty an' she seemed to do all the talkin'. She told Willie that they was the Devil's daughters. So Willie told her what had happened an' he was afeard 'f he wasn't at the Devil's house by night his head was goin' to be on the spear.

So the pretty girl got out a solid gold needle an' told Willie to pluck on the point of it three times with his finger an' he'd have wings. So Willie plucked on the point of the needle three times an' he had wings an' him an' the girls flew away. They jis riz right up like birds an' flew away. The girl told him to light out from the Devil's house a piece an' come on in a-walkin'.

So Willie done what she said. He lit an' went on up walkin' an' the girls flew right on up to the house. Willie seed the Devil settin' under a shade tree in front of the house an' he went up an' spoke to him. The Devil told him to git a seat an' that he seed he'd kept his word.

After while the girl come out an' said come on to supper. They got up an' went in an' Willie had never seed sich a table set in all his life. Jis ever'thing an' anything one could think of. In talkin' he mentioned God an' the very minute he said it ever'thing was gone off of the table an' there wasn't a thing there but a bowl of dishwater. The Devil jis got up an' walked out of the house 'thout say'n a word. The girl spoke to Willie. She said, "you musn't ever mention God's name. From now on there won't be anything on the table when you set down but dishwater, but you can wish for sump'n better as you set down an' hit'll be thar."

Then the girl told Willie that the Devil meant to kill him. All he wants is a good excuse for puttin' you out of the way. She said that the room he'd be put in to sleep had a spear bed in it. That was a bed with sharp spears under it stickin' up an' when anyone laid down on it they'd push up through an' kill 'em. But, the girl told him, when you go to git in the bed jis wish fer sump'n better an' you'll have a good bed. So Willie done like she told him an' he had a good bed an' slept well an' next mornin' he was settin' before the fire chawin' terbacker when the Devil come in. The Devil told him he was goin' away that day an' that his great-grandmother's granny had lost her solid gold ring in the well one time an' he wanted him to draw out the water an' git it that day, an' 'f he didn't have it when he come in that his head would go on a spear.

John Martin Kilgore and family of Wise. Mr. Kilgore told "Willie and the Devil" (No. 6-C). Photo from the James Taylor Adams Papers, John Cook Wyllie Library, Clinch Valley College, Wise, Virginia.

So Willie went out an' found the well about one third full of water. He got a bucket an' started drawin', but the more he drawed out the fuller hit got an' by the time the girl come an' said dinner was ready the well was runnin' over. He said no he couldn't come to no dinner then for he had to git that water out an' find that ring or his head would be on the spear that night shore. She told him to come on an' eat his dinner an' after dinner she'd go back an' help him. So he went on in an' there wasn't anything on the table but a bowl of dishwater, but he wished fer sump'n better an' the table was jist loaded with all sorts of good things. So after dinner the girl went back with him to the well an' she took a little solid gold dipper an' dipped out three dipperfuls an' the well was empty an' Willie clum down an' found the ring. An' that night he give it to the Devil an' he took hit without a word.

The next mornin' the Devil started off an' told Willie that his great-grandmother's granny lost her thimble in the stable a long time ago an' he wanted him to throw out the litter an' find hit that day an' 'f he didn't have [it] by the time he come in that night his head would go on the spear. So Willie took a shevel an' went out to the stable. Wasn't much litter in the stable an' he sot in shevelin' hit out, but the more he sheveled the more thar was, an' by the time the girl come out an' told him to come to dinner, the stable was runnin' over with litter. He told the girl he couldn't possibly come to dinner fer 'f he didn't find that thimble by night his head would be on the spear shore. But she told him to come on an' she'd go back an' help 'im after dinner. So he went on an' eat an' after dinner she took a little solid gold shevel an' went with him. She jis sheveled three shevelfulls an' the stable was as clean as your han'. An' they looked around an' found the thimble an' that night when the Devil come in Willie handed it to him. He took it without sayin' a word.

The third mornin' when the Devil started off he took Willie down below the house an showed him a big flat rock. He said that he wanted a two-story house with twenty-four rooms built on that big rock an' that he wanted it built of stone an' furnished ready to live in that night, an' 'f hit wasn't ready his head would go on the spear. Willie didn't know what to do, but he got an' old rock axe an' started in, but the more he worked the bigger the stone got an' when the girl called him to dinner he didn't have as much as one stone ready. He told her no he couldn't come. 'F he didn't have that house built by night his head would shore be on the spear. She told him to come on an' eat an' she'd go back with 'im after dinner an' he'p 'im some. So he went on an' eat dinner, an' after dinner the girl got a little solid gold axe an' went back with him an' struck on the flat rock three times an' thar stood a two-story stone house with twenty-four rooms all ready to live in. Now, she told Willie, "when the Devil comes in tonight, you show him the house an he'll like it, but after he starts on you fall back fifteen steps an' the house will disappear."

So that evenin' when the Devil come in Willie took him through the house an' he was well pleased with it. The Devil started on to supper an' Willie stopped till he was fifteen steps ahead of him an' he called the Devil an' they looked back an' the house was gone. No sign of it. The Devil was mad, but Willie told him that he'd said build the house. He hadn't said anything about lettin' hit stand.

The next mornin' the Devil went off, but he didn't say anything about Willie doin' anything that day. He hadn't been gone but a little while till the girl told Willie that fer him to go to the stable an' catch the poorest horse an' poorest mule he could find an' bring them down to the stile block in front of the house an' they'd go an' git married. Willie was right in for that. So he done what she said. Got out to the stable an' thar stood the poorest, boniest mule he'd ever seed an' a horse that was a good match fer him. So he bridled 'em an' led them down to the stile blocks an' the girl come out an' throwed a saddle on the mule an' he was the fattest finest mule he'd ever laid eyes on, an' jis rarin' an' pitchin' he was so full of life, an' when she saddled the hoss he was the same way.

So the girl got on the mule an' told Willie to get on the hoss an' away they went. Went on about a half a day an' Willie looked back an' seed the Devil a-comin' jis as hard as he could tare. The girl told Willie to jump off his hoss an' get a gravel an' put hit in her mule's ear. He did an' all at once all behind them was jis big rocks, cliffs an' boulders. The Devil had to go back to git tools to move 'em with an' they got another start on him. But after while Willie looked back an' seed him comin' again. The girl told Willie to jump off his mule [hoss] an' pick a thorn an' put it in her mules ear. He did an' all at once all behind them was the awfulest thorn thicket they had ever seed. So the Devil had to stop an' go back to git tools to cut 'em down with an' they got a right smart start on him again. But after a while Willie looked back an' seed him a-comin'. The girl told him to jump down an' take her thimble an' dip hit up full of water an' dash it in her mule's ear. Willie done what she told him an' all at once all the country they'd passed through was a sea of water. The Devil didn't like water an' he turned back. They went on an' got married an' went back an' took possession of ever'thing. The Devil never showed up an' the last time I heard of 'em they was gittin' long pretty well.

Collected by James Taylor Adams on January 20, 1942, from John Martin Kilgore of Wise, Virginia. He heard it from his father about 1880.

7 / *Jack and the Beggar*

I USED TO HEAR DAD TELL about a boy named Jack that lived by hisse'f. He said that one day a little beggar come to Jack's house an' Jack took him an' kep' him an' was good to him. Not long after the beggar went away Jack was waked up one night by somethin' on his porch, jes draggin' backards an' fer'rds from one en' of the porch to the tother. He got up an' looked out an' thar was a big dog draggin' a dead sheep across the porch. He went out an' the dog snuck off an' left the sheep a-layin' thar. But nex' mornin' the dog come in an' took up with 'im. He tried to run it off, but it wouldn't go, an' jes hung aroun'. Not long aiter that some robbers come one night an' tried to break in on Jack, but the dog chased 'em off. So Jack he was good to the dog aiter that. Then it wasn't long tell he drug in another sheep an' the neighbors seed it an' accused Jack of stealin' their sheep. Hit went on an' finally the dog went off an' didn't come back. Jack looked an' looked for him, but couldn't fin' him. One night he was settin' on his porch wonderin' what had become of his dog when he looked way back in the mountain an' seed a little light. Somehow he thought it was beckonin' for him to come. He went an' when he got there the light disappeared an' he found he was in a cave. He looked aroun' an' there on the floor of the cave was the skeleton of a dog. Well, he thought that was the skeleton of his dog. So he went back home. The nex' night he was settin' out on his porch an' he looked an' thar was the light ag'in. He got up an' went to it ag'in. This time he looked for the skeleton, but hit wasn't thar. Somebody had moved it. Then the nex' night he was settin' out on his porch an' he looked an' thar was that light ag'in. He went to it ag'in. When he got thar that time he didn't see no sign of anything. But he went furder back in the cave. All at once he seed a light way on ahead. He followed it an' hit kep' goin' an' goin' an' soon it come out at another place in a rough country an' thar was a little log house. The light went right on in the house an' Jack was afraid, but he followed it. When he opened the door thar set the beggar he'd took in on a big ches'. He got up an' pulled back the led an' in the chest was thousands an' thousands of dollars in gol' an' silver. He tol' Jack that he'd been murdered fer his money, but they never found it. An' that his spirit had come back to lead 'im to it. Because he'd took in a poor beggar an' a homeless dog he'd give it all to him. The big dog was thar, too. Then they both jes disappeared an' left Jack standin' thar by hisse'f with the ches' full of money.

Collected by James Taylor Adams on September 16, 1941, from Mrs. Edna Carter of Big Laurel, Virginia. She learned it from her father Patton Kilgore about 1920. This tale combines Motifs E 231, "Return from Dead to Reveal Murder," and E 371, "Return from Dead to Reveal Hidden Treasure."

8 / *Jack and the Devil*

ONE TIME THERE WAS A BOY named Jack. Jack was a poor boy, but he saved a few pennies now and then until by the time he was twenty-one and free he had a hundred dollars saved up. So he started out to seek his fortune and find something to invest his money in.

So Jack he went on and on until one day he was going down the road when he met up with the Devil.

"Where you goin', Jack?" said the Devil.

"Oh, I'm jis goin' out to seek my fortune and find sump'n to invest my money in," said Jack.

"Well," said the Devil, "I've got a hundred dollars, too. Why don't we put our money together and go into business?"

"That'ud suit me exactly," said Jack.

So Jack and the Devil put their money together and then they begin to consider what they'd go in to.

"There ort to be good money in farming," said the Devil, "Lets raise corn. You know people have to have corn."

"All right," said Jack, "that suits me."

So they got 'em some land and planted a big field of corn. Oh it growed off jis fine an' before it was time to gather it the Devil said, "Now we'll have to figure out some way to divide our crop. Tell you what I'll do, Jack. I'll take what grows under the ground and you can have what grows on top. You see I'm sort of an underground feller anyhow."

"All right," said Jack, "that suits me."

So that fall when they gathered their crop Jack got all the corn and fodder an' the Devil got nothin' but the roots. But he was a game feller an' took it without any kick.

The next year they decided to raise taters. Before time to gather 'em the Devil said he believed he would take what growed on top of the ground. So they agreed that way an' when they dug the taters Jack got all the taters and the Devil had nothin' left but the tops. But he was a game sort of feller an' raised no kick about it.

So the next year they agreed to go into the hog raising business. They got a whole lot of sows and a few boars an' let 'em loose in a big field. Oh, they growed off fine and then they brought pigs an' they growed an' hit wudn't long till they had the field plum full of fine hogs.

Now the Devil was runnin' short of money an' he saw [that he'd] have to divide the hogs so he could sell his share an' [have money] to start ag'in on. So they figured out a way to divide ['em. They] agreed to git in the field an' each one could have the [hogs he could] catch n' throw over the fence in another joinin' field. [That's] what they done. Oh, hit took 'em two or three days to catch [and] throw 'em all over. But at last they had 'em all throwed [over and] neither one of 'em could figure or count so they had [no way of] tellin' which hogs each one had throwed over. So they [didn't know] how they'd ever tell their hogs apart. Jack had an idea [then]. "Look here, ever' hog I throwed over I jerked a [quile in its tail"]. So they got over an' looked and ever' hog had [a quile in its tail].

Collected by James Taylor Adams on November 23, 1941, from Gaines Kilgore, Wise County, Virginia. Collected in the Wise Owl Cafe. Gaines heard the tale from his father. A combination of Type 1030, "The Crop Division," and Type 1036, "Hogs with Curly Tails." See Chase, Grandfather Tales. Chase recorded a version of this tale from Gaines Kilgore on January 28, 1950. The recording is in the Archive of Folk Culture (Library of Congress Number AFS 19,046 (19,080, Side B2). Title of this version is WILLIE (BOBTAIL) AND THE DEVIL.

9 / *Jack and the Giant*

ONE TIME THERE WAS A MAN AND WOMAN had four boys. The youngest boy was marked and was half boy and half dog. They called him Jack. I never heard what they called the other three. So the old man and old woman died out an' the four boys fixed up an' struck out to seek their fortunes.

So they went on an' on an' on. They got tired of travelin' an' they come to an old layin' out house an' axed a man 'f hit'ud be all right fer them to stay in it a while. He said yes that he owned the place but they wouldn't stay in it. Nobody could live there 'cause hit was hainted or sump'n. But they was tired out an' they told him they'd try it. He said all right 'f they'd stay there he'd give 'em a deed to it.

So they took up. That night they built 'em a big roarin' fire an' the three oldest boys went to bed an' Jack was settin' up on the hathe with his head in his hands like he was thinkin'. One of his brothers says, "What you thinkin' 'bout, Jack?" He sayd, "I'uz jis thinkin' 'bout that big fat hog we seed up the road yanner an' believe I'll go an' git it."

So he pulled out an' after while in he come with it. The next day Jack an' his two oldest brothers went off to work an' that night when they come back the youngest brother an' the hog was gone. They hunted everywhere, but couldn't find 'em.

So they give up.

That night the two oldest brothers went to bed an' left Jack settin' on the hathe with his head in his hands like he was thinkin'. "What ye thinkin' 'bout, Jack?" one of 'em axed him. "Oh, I'uz jis thinkin' 'bout a fine fat steer I seed today. Think I'll go an' git him." So off he went an' soon he come back with the steer.

The next day him an' his oldest brother went off to work. That night when they come back their other brother was gone an' the steer was gone too.

That night the oldest boy went to bed an' left Jack settin' on the hathe with his head in his hands like he was thinkin'. The oldest boy said, "What ye thinkin' 'bout, Jack?" Jack said, "I was thinkin' 'bout a fine sheep I seed in the pasture today as we come home. Think I'll go an' git it." So off he went an' soon he was back with the sheep.

The next day Jack went off to work an' left his oldest brother there to take care of the house. When he come home that night his brother an' the mutton was gone. He searched everywhere but couldn't find 'em.

So that night Jack was settin' there by hisself wonderin' what had become of his three brothers an' what would happen to him, when all at once he heard sump'n like somebody takin' on an' a scratchin' and clawin' in the big chist that sat ag'inst the wall. He was scared an' started to run, but he decided to investigate an' he prized up the led an' there was a pretty girl in the chist. He helped her out an' she tol' Jack that a big giant lived in an old house in the woods not far away an' that he'd put her in the chist an' brought her there an' that he'd give her a sleepin' dram an' she'd jis waked up. The giant she said had told her he was goin' to kill her. So Jack he figured it all out. The old giant thought he'd killed the girl an' was goin' to let him find her body there an' he'd run off he thought.

So Jack told the girl to stay there an' do jis what he tol' her an' they'd git even with the giant.

So Jack he went an' watched where the girl said the giant lived an' seed him comin' home with three cows on his back.

Gee, he was big an' strong.

So Jack he come back an' tol' the girl to go with him. So that night Jack took the girl an' let her stand in the path where the giant would be travelin'. When he seed her he thought she was a haint an' he fell down an' prayed fer her not to kill him. She jis stood an' looked straight at him like Jack told her to do. At last she said 'f he'd show her what he'd done with Jack's three brothers an' give her a bushel of gold an' leave the country she would go away n' never bother him any more. He agreed an' he took her an' went down in a cave where he had Jack's brothers all penned up to fatten. Bones of other people he'd killed an' eat lay scattered all about. So he turned them loose an' give her a bushel of gold an' got his stuff together an' left the country, an' the girl an' Jack got married an' that very day he got rid of his mark an' was jis like anybody else. An' his brothers they married Jack's wife's sisters an' they all lived happy.

Collected by James Taylor Adams on November 12, 1941, from Mrs. Bethel Lee Adams of Big Laurel, Virginia. She learned it from Ivory Jacobs in Knott County, Kentucky.

10 / Jack and the Giant

ONE TIME THERE WAS A YOUNG MAN named Jack who was traveling through the country. He stopped at a house to stay all night and noticed that the house had a tall fence built all around it and that the men put a big lock on the gate before they went to bed. The next morning he asked the man why he had his house fenced in with such a strong fence and he told him there was a big giant in the neighborhood and that he would turn himself into all sorts of things and kill and steal from the neighbors. It was common, said the man, for a whole family to be killed at night and all their property carried off.

Now Jack was a strong young man and quite a fighter, and he was pretty good at working out things. So he went around over the neighborhood and talked with the people and they said they would give him a thousand dollars if he would kill the old giant.

So Jack he set to work and built a fence made out of the biggest logs he could find. Oh they were trees three feet through. He took in about an acre, never paying any attention to the giant who would swoop down on the neighborhood nearly every night and carry off a cow or oxen.

Well, at last they had the fence made and Jack told the people all to bring their stock and put them in the pen. They did, but wondered what good that was going to do for Jack insisted that they leave the gate partly open with some bars to keep the cattle in. But Jack told them he wanted the giant to go in at the gate and he would slam the gate shut and have him. "Oh," they all said, "that won't do any good. He can turn himself to a squirrel, a mouse or even a worm and come right out." "That's all right," said Jack, "just let him try it."

So they put all their stock in the pen and Jack set to watch the gate. Nothing happened for two or three nights, but one night way long about midnight Jack heard a thundering and rumbling up the mountain and here come the old giant. He walked right in at the gate straddled over the bars and caught an oxen and was about to come out when Jack and some men he had with him slammed the gate shut. And just as soon as they closed the gate Jack opened a little gate just big enough for him to squeeze through and went in. Just as he went in he saw the giant drop the oxen and all at once he just sank down and there stood a little mouse and it made a dash for a hole in the fence, but Jack was too quick for him and stomped the mouse and there lay the old giant mashed all to pieces. And Jack got his thousand dollars and went on to seek his fortune.

Collected by James Taylor Adams on March [rest of date torn], from Drady Bolling of Flat Gap, Virginia. She learned it from her mother.

11 / *Jack Goes to Seek His Fortune*

ONE TIME THERE WAS A LITTLE BOY named Jack. His mother was dead and his father had married again, and his step-mother didn't like Jack and was mean to him.

So one day Jack decided he would leave home and go out in the world and seek his fortune. So he started out. He hadn't gone but a little piece when he met a horse.

"Good morning, Jack," said the horse, "where are you going?"

"Going to seek my fortune," said Jack.

"May I go with you?" said the horse.

"Yes," said Jack, "the more the merrier." So Jack and the horse went on.

Hadn't gone but a little piece till they met a cow.

"Good morning, Jack," said the cow,"where are you going?"

"Going to seek my fortune," said Jack.

"May I go with you?" said the cow.

"Yes," said Jack, "the more the merrier." So Jack and the horse and the cow went on.

Hadn't gone but a little piece till they met a dog.

"Good morning, Jack," said the dog, "where are you going?"

"Going to seek my fortune," said Jack.

"May I go with you?" said the dog.

"Yes," said Jack, "the more the merrier." So Jack and the horse and the cow and the dog went on.

Hadn't gone but a little piece till they met a ram.

"Good morning, Jack," said the ram, "where are you going?"

"Going to seek my fortune," said Jack.

"May I go with you?" said the ram.

"Yes," said Jack, "the more the merrier." So Jack and the horse and the cow and the dog and the ram went on.

Hadn't gone but a little piece till they met a rooster.

"Good morning, Jack," said the rooster, "where are you going?"

"Going to seek my fortune," said Jack.

"May I go with you?" said the rooster.

"Yes," said Jack, "the more the merrier." So Jack and the horse and the cow and the dog and the ram and the rooster went on.

Hadn't gone but a little piece till they met a cat.

"Good morning, Jack," said the cat, "where are you going?"

"Going to seek my fortune," said Jack.

"May I go with you?" said the cat.

"Yes," said Jack, "the more the merrier. So Jack and the horse and the cow and the dog and the ram and the rooster and the cat went on.

Hadn't gone but a little piece till they met a goose.

"Good morning, Jack," said the goose, "where are you going?"

"Going to seek my fortune," said Jack.

"May I go with you?" said the goose.

"Yes," said Jack, "the more the merrier." So Jack and the horse and the cow and the dog and the ram and the rooster and the cat and the goose went on.

They went on and on; traveled all day. Long about sundown they begin to look for a place to stay all night. They was in an awful wild and thinly settled country and hadn't seen nobody for a long time. At last they come to a big house settin' way up on the side of a hill with a big high fence around it. They went up to the house and found that nobody lived there and decided to put up in it for the night.

So Jack put the horse just inside the gate, the cow just outside and told them to not let anyone come in. Then he put the ram on the porch and the goose just inside the door and the cat on the hearth and the dog under the bed and the rooster up on top of the house, and pulled off his things and went to bed.

It was a robber's meeting place, but Jack didn't know it. The robbers had stored a lot of money there they had robbed people of in the country and towns around there.

So 'way long in the night the robbers come. They thought somebody might be around so two of them waited down the road a little piece and sent the other one to investigate. He slipped up to the gate and just as he got there the cow picked him up on her horns and tossed him over the gate. The horse kicked him onto the porch. The ram butted him through the door. The goose flapped him with her wings and bit him. He run to the fireplace to make a light and the cat scratched him. He run under the bed and the dog bit him. And as he jumped through the window and started running the rooster begin crowing for day.

When the feller got back to his buddies he was nearly dead. They wanted to know what was the matter. He told them he slipped up to the gate and there was a farmer there and pitched him over the gate on a pitchfork; a blacksmith over there struck him with a sledgehammer and knocked him onto the porch. A railmaker there struck him with his mawl and knocked him through the door. There stood a thrasherman and he liked to flailed him to death with his flail. He run over to the fireplace to start a light and there was an old woman setting on the hearth a sewing and she stuck her needle in him. He went to hide under the bed, but there was a shoemaker under there and he stuck his awl in him. He made it to the window and jumped out and as he ran away he heard the leader of them all up on top of the house hollering, "When you get through with him send him up to me-ee." So the robber's was afraid to go back to the house and next morning Jack looked over the place and found their gold. He took it and bought hay for the horse and cow; bones for the dog; milk for the cat; and corn for the ram and the goose and rooster. Then Jack married him a wife and they all lived happy.

Collected by James Taylor Adams on November 15, 1940 from Lenore Corene Kilgore. She learned it from her grandmother, Mrs. Letty Mays, about 1925. Type 130, "The Animals in Night Quarters." See Chase, Jack Tales, *JACK AND THE ROBBERS.*

12 / Jack Goes to Seek His Fortune

ONE TIME THERE WAS A BOY named Jack. His daddy owned a small farm and had give Jack some calves to raise for his own. When the calves got up a right smart size Jack took 'em to market and sold 'em an' bought him a horse an' buggy an' got in the buggy an' started off to seek his fortune. He'd spent his last penny fer the hoss an' buggy an' a good pistol an' pocket knife to protect hisse'f with.

Jack drove on in his buggy. Come to a house that looked like good livers lived there and he might git to stay all night. He hollered at the gate an' a girl come out an' axed him what he wanted. He told her that he was travlin' an' would like to git to stay all night. She told him they couldn't keep him. Said her father was dead an' that her married sister who lived over the hill a little piece had taken sick an' sent fer her mother to come an' set up with 'er an' they wudn't nobody there but her an' her younger sister an' the niggers. Jack was about to drive on when the younger sister come out n' started beggin' her older sister to let 'im stay. She finally agreed to let him stay. So he turned his hoss an' buggy over to the niggers an' went on in. That night after supper the oldest girl said that bein' there was nobody at home but jis them two girls she guess they'd better lock 'im in his room. He agreed an' they showed 'im his room an' after he'd gone in they locked the door on 'im.

'Way long in the night he was waked up by a racket goin' on in the house. He listened an' could tell by the girls screams that somebody was brakin' in on 'em. He broke his door down an' run out with his pistol in one han' an' his knife in tother. The girls was screamin' that the niggers was breakin' in on 'em. He jis seed two men. One of 'em was chokin' the oldest girl an' the other'n was makin' for the youngest. He cut loose with his pistol an' shot at one of 'em an' whacked at the other an' cut his han' off. He run, but the one he shot fell dead right there. After they'uz sort o' quited down Jack axed fer a pan of water, an' started washing the dead man. He was not a nigger, but a white man with his face an' hands blacked. The han' was a white

60

man's han' too.

The girls tol' Jack the dead man looked a sight like their brother-in-law, but hit wasn't him. So Jack got out an' takin' the girls with him in his buggy he went to their sister's [house]. They found her husband in bed. Their mother said her son-in-law had been hunting an' fell on an axe an' cut his han' off. [So Jack] had took the han' along an' he took it out of his pocket [and held] hit up an' axed 'em if that was his han'. They seed that [hit was]. Hit all come out that the brother-in-law an' his brother [made] up to rob the girls an' had sent word that the married girl [was] sick in order to git their mother away from home.

Collected by James Taylor Adams on November 23, 1941, from Gaines Kilgore in Wise, Virginia. Gaines heard his father tell this tale a few years before.

13 / *Jack and the Robbers*

ONE TIME THERE WAS A BOY named Jack and one day he slipped off from home and struck out to seek his fortune. He went on and on until it was getting nearly dark. He come up to a big house and hollered and a girl come to the door and asked him what he wanted. He told her he was a traveling and was looking for a place to stay all night. She said she couldn't keep him, but Jack he was tired and so he told her he just had to stay and walked right in. She tried to get him to leave, but Jack wouldn't go. Finally she said, "Well, all right. If you won't go you won't go." Then she said," Let us play some games. Let's see who can jump the furtherest." So Jack agreed. She said for him to stand in the door and jump first. He did and as he jumped she slammed the door shut and bolted hit and he couldn't get back in.

So he went on and on. It was black dark now. He come to an old deserted mill. He went in and looked around for some place to lay down. Best place he could find was the mill hopper. So he crawled up in it.

After a while Jack heard somebody talking. Then some robbers come in and set down right under the hopper to count their money. He lay right still for awhile, but he wanted to see them so bad that he at last sort of raised up to peep over when down went the hopper right among the robbers. They was so scared they all jumped up and run off, leaving their money a-laying there.

Jack he got up and gathered up the money and put it in one of the sacks he found there and struck out for home.

Collected by James Taylor Adams on November 20, 1940, from Mary Carter. She learned it about 1890 from her mother, Elizabeth Roberts Adams. Type 1653, "The Robbers Under the Tree."

14 / Jack the Woodchopper

ONE TIME THEY WAS AN OLD WOMAN and she had three sons. The youngest son was named Jack and Jack was a good boy, but his brothers were mean and didn't like to mind their mother. Now this old woman was a widow and awful poor.

They kept getting poorer and poorer all the time. So the old woman told the oldest boy he'd have to go into the forest and cut wood and sell it to get something for them to live on. He didn't want to go, but he finally went off muttering, carrying a piece of cake and a bottle of wine, nearly the last the old woman had.

So he went on tell he come to an old man settin' on a log. He was very old and looked awful hungry. He said, "My boy, won't you divide your food with me?" "No sir, I've only got a piece of cake and a bottle of wine and come to think of it I'm hungry." So he eat his cake and drunk his wine and the old man settin' there watching him and never offered him a bite. He went on and started chopping wood and the first tree fell on him and broke his legs and they had to come and carry him home a cripple for life.

So the old woman sent her second son. He went off mut-

tering to himself, and carrying the last piece of cake and last bottle of sweet wine. He went on till he come to where the old man
was settin' on a log. The old man hailed him and said, "My boy,
won't you give me a little of your cake and wine. I'm awful hungry." "I have nothing to spare beggars," the boy said, and he eat
his cake and drank his wine and started chopping wood. Hadn't
chopped but a few licks till he cut his foot and was carried home
a cripple for life.

So the old woman said to her youngest boy, "Jack you'll
have to go and chop wood so we may have something to live
on." So Jack started out, but all he had to take with him was a
crust of bread and a few sups of sour wine in a bottle. So he
went on and found the old man settin' on the log. "Give me
something to eat, my boy, I'm starving," the old man said to Jack.
So Jack he was tender-hearted and he gave the old man half of
his crust and half of his wine and as soon as he took it his part
and Jack's turned into a fine cake and a full bottle of sweet wine
and they had a good meal. Then the old man pointed to a tree
and told Jack if he would chop away the roots he would find
something that would bring him good luck all his days. So Jack
he chopped away the roots of the tree and found a golden goose.

So Jack he took the golden goose and started home. Hadn't
gone far till he met up with three girls. One of them ran up and
started to stroke the goose and she stuck to it and couldn't git
loose. Another one of the girls tried to pull her loose and she
stuck to her and the other one tried to pull her loose and she
stuck to her. So they started out Jack carrying his goose and the
girls following behind him.

So they went and met up with three preachers. One of them
began shaming the girls for following a poor woodchopper, and
told them to leave him and come with them to church.
They kept right on after Jack and the old preacher walked up
and laid his hand on the last girl's shoulder and his hand stuck
to her and he started on after them. The other two preachers
began calling for him to come on with them and one ran up
and grabbed him by the shoulder and his hand stuck to him
and the other grabbed him and he stuck to him, so they all

went on following Jack and his golden goose.

So they all went on and had to pass the King's house. Now the King had a daughter who had never smiled and he had offered to let her marry any man that would make her smile. So this girl was standing at her window looking out and saw Jack pass by leading all these people behind his golden goose and it looked so funny that she smiled. The old King thought Jack had done that to make her smile so he sent for Jack to come in. And when Jack went in he told him he'd made his daughter smile, but before he let him marry her, there was one more thing he had to do. He would have to find somebody that would eat a thousand loaves of bread at one time. So Jack he thought that would be impossible. So he left and went out in the woods. There he found a man setting on a log with all kinds of bread scraps layin' around him. He was just tightning up his belt. He told Jack he'd eat all the bread he could find and was still hungry. So Jack told him to come and go with him and he took him to the King's house and there all stacked up was a thousand loaves. The man started in on 'em and eat 'em all up right now.

So the old King called Jack in and told him that there was one more thing he'd have to do before he'd let him marry his daughter. He'd have to find somebody that could drink a thousand bottles of wine at one time. So Jack thought it would be impossible to find such a man and he went off in the woods. There he found a man with parched lips setting by the path and all sort of wine bottles lying empty around him. He told Jack he'd drunk all the wine he could find, but he could not quench his thirst. So Jack told him to follow him and he took him to the old King's house and there was a thousand bottles of wine and this fellow drunk them right down. So the old King told Jack there was one more thing he'd have to do before he'd let him marry his daughter. He'd have to find a ship that would sail on both land and water. Well, Jack thought that was impossible. So he left and went out in the woods. There he met up with the old man that had gave him the golden goose. He said, "What troubles you, Jack?" And Jack told him he had to find a ship that would sail on land as well as on water before the old King would give him his daughter for a wife. So the old man took out his knife and started whitling. In no time he had whittled out a ship. The ship started growing and right away it was a big ship. Jack got in it and it sailed away over the land and across rivers and come to the King's house. When the old King saw him and his ship he gave him his daughter and they were married and sailed away across the ocean. They was gone several years and when they went back the old King was dead and Jack become King and his wife was the Queen and they lived happy.

Collected by James Taylor Adams on October 30, 1941, from Spencer Adams, who learned it from Thomas Countiss of Flat Gap, Virginia. Thomas learned the tale from his father Schuyler Countiss. A Combination of Type 513A, "Six Go Through the Whole World," and Type 513B, "The Land and Water Ship."

15-A / **Jack's Goose**

ONE TIME THERE WAS TWO BROTHERS named Jack and Will. And one night they made up to go away out in the woods and camp. They started out and after going through a lot of woods they come up on an old abandoned house. Didn't look like anybody had lived there for years and years; and years and years.

So Jack and Will went in and looked about and couldn't find any sign that anybody had been there for a long time. So they decided to stay there that night. Now as they come along that evening they passed a big flock of geese and they had caught one which they was a-going to roast for their supper. So they picked the goose and cleaned it and put it up on some sticks before the fire they had built, to roast.

Will, who was the oldest and biggest of the brothers, told Jack for him to roast the goose and have it ready and he'd go back the way they had come and catch another goose and they'd have a regular feast.

So Will went on off and Jack he kept chunking up the fire and roasting the goose.

All at once he heard a noise at the door and he looked and there stood an old gray-bearded man leaning on a cane. He said, "Oo-oo-I'm freezin' to death."

"Come in, granddaddy, an' have a warm," Jack told him.

The old man hobbled in and set down before the fire and never said another word.

After while he said, "Whu-u-up! Suck all the skin off of Jack's goose; whu-u-up! suck him up." And Jack seen all the brown baked skin on his goose just slip off and was gone.

"If you do that again, granddaddy, I'll biff you," said Jack.

The old man set there for a little while and then—

"Whu-u-up! suck all the skin off of Jack's goose; whu-u-up, suck him up." And this time all the meat went off the goose and there was nothing left but just the frame of bones hanging there on the sticks. So Jack he drawed back and biffed the old man. But the old feller jumped on Jack and knocked him down and stuck his beard in him and liked to killed him. When Jack come to the old man was gone.

In a little while Will come in with another goose and found Jack laying there groaning and taking on. He asked Jack what was the matter and he told him. But Will didn't believe him and told him he had just eat up all the goose and it had made him sick, and that he was going to get rid of him. So Will gathered Jack up and took him out in the back yard and there was a pit there and he throwed Jack in. Then he roasted the other goose and eat it, laid down and slept till morning and went back home and told Jack was lost in the woods.

Collected by James Taylor Adams on August 29, 1940, from his wife, Dicy Adams. She learned it from her mother about 1900. This tale— particularly the B version— bears some resemblance to Type 301A, "Quest for a Vanished Princess."

15-B / *Suck All the Skin Off Jack's Goose*

ONE TIME THAR'UZ THREE BROTHERS named Will, Tom an' Jack. Will was the oldest an' Jack was the baby boy.

They'd heard thar was some gold hid somewheres an' they started out to look for it. One night they put up in an' old house an' Will and Tom went out to look for the gold an' left Jack to rustle up sumpin' for supper. He got out an' found a goose an' killed hit an' put it on a stick an' set it up before the fire to roast. Hit hadn't been long tell an old raggedy man come to the door an' said, "Ooh, I'm freezin'." "Come in, granddaddy," said Jack, "an' warm yourse'f." He come in an' set down by the fire an' warmed his hans. All at once he said, "swoop" an' all the skin flew off of Jack's goose. "Do that ag'in, granddaddy," said Jack, "an' I'll biff ye." "Swoop, suck all the skin off o' Jack's goose," he said, "swoop, suck 'im up." An' all the meat was gone leaving jes the bones hangin' thar. Jack made fer 'im an' he run an' Jack after him. All at once Jack's feet went out from under 'im an' down into a hole he went. Down in thar he found the old man an' he was rich an' had all that gold they was lookin' for. "I know I done ye wrong, Jack," the old man said, "an' I'm goin' to make up to ye by givin' ye all the gold an' yore choice of my three daughters. So Jack took the prettiest girl an' the old man give 'im the gold an' he got out an' thar was Will an' Tom waitin' for him. They wanted the gold an' the girl too. They tied up Jack an' got him in a boat with the girl an' all started across the river. The girl slipped an' untied Jack an' about that time Will an' Tom got into a fight over the girl an' turned the boat over. They each one had half of the gold tied around his waist. They couldn't swim an' went down an' drowned and Jack swum to the bank with the girl an' they married an' was happy without the gold.

Collected by James Taylor Adams on May 21, 1941, from Finley Adams.

16 / The Jack's Head

ONCE THERE WERE THREE BOYS named Jack, Tom and Harry. Their mother died and their father married again. The step-- mother didn't like them and made up her mind to get rid of them. So one day their father had to go away from home and the step-mother made the boys sleep out in the barn that night. Long in the night they seen her coming with a shovel full of fire. They slipped out and went upon the hill and watched her put the fire in the hayloft and run back to the house. Soon the barn was burning down and the boys knowing she would find some other means of killing them struck out to leave the country.

Tom was the oldest boy and after they had traveled awhile they came to a road with three forks. Tom told the boys they could take choice of roads and he would take the one left.

So the boys parted. Tom soon found a place to stay with a rich farmer. After while he noticed a fine house on another farm and asked the man he was staying with why nobody lived there. He told him a man had been killed there or rather he disap- peared and they couldn't find him and he had bought the place from his heirs. He said he'd give it to Tom if he'd stay in three nights. Tom told him he'd do it.

So Tom took a Bible and went to the house one night and made him on a fire and set down to read. After a while he heard something and looked up and there came a man without any head on coming down the stairs. He came right up and stood by Tom but didn't say anything. Tom didn't say anything either. Then he went back upstairs and Tom laid down and slept the rest of the night.

Next morning Tom heard the man outside hollering for him. He waited till he'd hollered three times and then answered. He came in and asked Tom how he'd faired and Tom told him what he'd seen.

The next night it was the same way, except when the man came down stairs he was carrying his head in his hands. He didn't speak nor did Tom. And that morning the man came and called for Tom three times before he answered and he came in and Tom told him what had happened.

The third night Tom was sitting there when he heard something being dragged over the floor upstairs. He looked up and there came the man dragging a coffin behind him and kicking his head along in front of him down the stairs. Tom was frightened that time. So when the man came up and stood by him he looked at him and said: "In the name of the father, son and holy ghost, what do you want?" The man told him he'd been killed there for his money and his body buried under the hearthrock. His money, he told Tom, was behind a certain board in the ceiling of the wall, and that he could have it if he'd take his bones and bury them. Tom told him he would, and he disappeared, saying he'd never be seen by any man again. So that morning when the man who Tom worked for came Tom told him what had happened and they raised the hearthrock and shore enough there was a skeleton under there. They took it to the graveyard and buried it and came back and found the loose plank and prized hit off and found a thousand dollars in gold and silver.

Tom had promised his brothers to meet them back at the place he'd left them in three years to a day. So now his time was up and the man gave him his pay and a deed for the house he'd stayed in, a horse and buggy, and his oldest girl for a wife. Tom and his wife got in their buggy and started off for the forks of the road to meet Jack and Harry. They got there and found nobody there. Wasn't long till they seen a boy coming up both the other roads. They hadn't done so well, but they had got by all right. They all got in Jack's [Tom's] carriage and struck out to visit their father.

They drove up in front of their father's house. They called and their father and step-mother came out. They wanted to stay all night, but their father said they hadn't kept nobody for three years, not since his three boys were burnt up in the barn. Tom asked his father if he'd know his boys if he was to see them. He said he didn't know, but he knew they were dead. Then he said that he would know Jack by him having a mark on his breast. Tom said, "Pull back your shirt, Jack, and show father the mark." The old man and his wife both liked to fainted. But he recovered and got a blacksnake whip and cut the old woman all to pieces. And after he whipped her good and plenty he sent her packing off.

Tom took his father and brothers back to his house with him. The boys married his wife's two sisters and their father lived with Tom. And the last time I was through that country they were all doing just fine.

Collected by James Taylor Adams on January 20, 1942, from 12-year-old Virginia Stallard. She learned the tale from her mother. A combination of Motif E 231, "Return from Dead to Reveal Murder," and Motif E 371, "Return from Dead to Reveal Hidden Treasure."

17 / *Soldier Jack and the Magic Sack*

ONE TIME THERE WAS A YOUNG MAN named Jack. Heard my pa tell this many an' many a time. Sometimes pa'd call 'im Jack Frost an' sometimes Soldier Jack.

Said that Jack had served a term in the King's army. Didn't git no pay in them days. When they turned him loose they give him nothin' but two loaves of light bread.

So Soldier Jack he hit out, tryin' to make his way back home or to seek his fortune wherever he might find it.

Hadn't went but a little piece tell he met up with an old bagger man. He bagged Jack to give 'im somethin' to eat. So Jack he was goodhearted an' he give the bagger one loaf of his light bread. An' then he went on. Hadn't gone but a little piece tell he met up with another ol' bagger man. He begin bagging Jack fer somethin' to eat an' Jack give 'im half of his loaf of light bread, an' started on.

Hadn't gone but a little piece tell he got to studyin'. He thought now I've not been fair with that last old bagger man. I give the fust one a whole loaf of light bread an' the last only a half a loaf. So he turned aroun' in the middle of the road an' run back tell he'd overtook the last ol' bagger an' he told him how he felt about it an' give 'im the other half of loaf of light bread.

The ol' bagger thanked 'im very kindly an' he said to Jack, he says, "You're sich a good kindhearted man that I'm goin' to give you sump'n." So he took a sack from across his shoulder an' a long slim glass from his pocket an' he give 'em to Jack an' said, "Now this sack is a magic sack. Anytime you want anything in the worl' to go in this sack all ye've got to do is jist slap the sack with one han' an' hold hit open with the tother an' what ye want to go in will go right in. An' this glass here will tell ye where a sick person is goin' to git well or die. All ye have to do is fill it full of clear spring water an' hol' hit up in front of the bed where the sick person's lyin'. 'F they're goin' to git well ye'll see the image of death standin' at the foot of the bed. But 'f they're goin' to die death will be standin' at the head of the bed."

So Jack, he took the sack and slung hit across his shoulder, an' he took the glass an' put hit in his pocket an' went on. He traveled on an' on all day. Late in the evenin' he was gittin' mighty hungry. He'uz goin' through a strip of woods an' looked up in a big tree an' seed six wild turkeys settin' on a limb. He thought, now 'f I could catch them turkeys I could swap 'em fer sump'n to eat. An' then he thought what the ol' bagger had said about the magic sack. So he held the mouth of hit open with one han' an' slapped on hit with the tother an' said:

"Whickety whack
Jump into my sack."

That's what the ol' bagger had said fer 'im to say, an' shore enough all the turkeys jis flew right down into his sack. They made 'im a right smart load, but he went on with 'em. Hadn't gone fer tell he come to a tavern. He offered them the turkeys fer a good night's lodgin' an' two dollars in money an' they took 'im up an' fixed 'im a good supper, give him a good bed that night an' a good breakfast nex' mornin'.

After breakfast he took his sack an' went on. Went on an' on. Gittin' late the nex' day when he come to a big fine house in a patch of woods. Nobody lived thar. He wondered why nobody'd live in sich a fine house as that. Oh, hit'uz a big house, fifteen or twenty rooms. Hadn't went fer tell he met a man in the road. "Say, my frien'," he said to the man, "why don't nobody live in this big fine house I jis passed back here a little piece?"

The man looked scared. "Oh," he said, "nobody can't live thar. Didn't ye know. That's a hainted house. They say hit's the home of the Devil."

Now Jack had been a soldier an' was tough. He didn't fear anything. Cared fer nothin'. So he said, "I'd stay thar." The man looked at him like he thought he'uz sort o' crazy. "Well," he said, "the man that owns hit lives up the road here in the next house. I guess he'd give ye the place to stay in it."

So Jack went on an' come to the next house. He hollered an' a man come out an' wanted to know who he was an' what he wanted. Jack told him he was Soldier Jack an' he'd like to stay in the big house he'd passed back thar a little piece. The man tol' him 'f he'd stay one night thar by hisse'f that he'd give him the house an' all the lan' aroun' hit an' throw him in a thousan' dollars in gold.

So Jack he went back to the house an' took up. He had some stuff to eat he'd bought with his turkey money.

He was settin' thar before the fire way long in the night an' in a sudden the door shoved open an' in walked three little black devils with sacks across their backs. "Hello, Soldier Jack," they said, "we heard you was here an' pappy sent us up with a half a bushel of gold a piece to play poker with ye." Jack jis had forty-two cents left of his turkey money, but he told 'em all right he'd gamble with ['em] as long as his money lasted. They said all right, an' they drawed up their cheers an' got out a deck of cards an' they went to gamblin'.

Jack was lucky right at the start. So they played on an' on, tell hit was after midnight an' Jack had won all the money they all had an' that was a bushel an' a half of gold.

Then the little black devils got mad. They started a disturbment. Said they'uz goin' to kill Jack 'f he didn't give 'em back their money. He wouldn't do it. They went off but come back in a little while with the old devil with 'em. He had a big firey sword an' he drawd' hit on Jack an' said he'uz goin' to cut his head off. Jack thought of his magic sack, but he doubted 'f hit'ud work on the Devil, but he thought he'd try it out on 'em. So he held open hit's mouth with one han' and slapped it with the other an' said:

"Whickety, Whack
Jump into my sack."

An' the ol' Devil and three little black devils all jis jumped into the sack an' scrooched down an' Jack tied 'em up an' sot 'em away in one corner.

So the next mornin' the man that owned the place come down an' invited Jack up fer breakfast an' he made him a deed to the house an' a thousan' acres aroun' hit an' give him a whole bushel of gol' to git started livin' on.

Jack didn't want to settle down jis then, so he jis locked his doors an' started out to see the worl'. Wherever he went he foun' everybody happy an' people would come to the road to 'im to axe him to come in an' eat with 'em or stay all night. An' he was good to everybody he met. He'd scatter gold pieces about to children an' give whole hand fulls of gold to people he thought was needin' it.

He was gone a month or two when one day he happened to think about leavin' the Devil and his three little black Devils tied up in his magic sack an' he decided they'd been punished enough an' that he ort to go an' turn 'em loose. So he went back home an' turned 'em loose an' they'uz mighty glad to git loose an' went runnin' off jis as hard as they could go.

So Jack locked up his doors ag'in an' he struck out ag'in. One day he heard that the King's daughter was awful bad off. They said he'd had all the best doctors in his kingdom with 'er but all of 'em had give her up. Said they wudn't no chance. An' they tol' Jack that the ol' King was so troubled an' mad that he'd cut off all the doctors' heads.

So Jack thought of his magic glass an' he said to hisse'f, "now, right here's a good place to try hit out." So he went up to the place where the King lived an' he went in an' tol' the King he believed he could tell fer a certainty where or not his daughter was goin' to live or die. Well, the ol' King, he'uz so troubled about his only daughter that he'uz willin' to try anything.

So the King tol' Jack to go ahead an' see 'f he could tell 'im. An' Jack he went in an' thar laid the girl jis wasted away to skin an' bones an' so bad off that she wudn't pay no 'tention to anybody. So Jack he called fer some clear spring water an' he filled his glass with hit an' helt hit up by the girl's bed an' looked through it an' shore enough thar stood Death at the head of her bed. So Jack he went out an' tol' the King his girl shore had to die. Death was standin' at the head of her bed. The ol' King was so mad when he heard that that he tol' his soldiers to grab holt of Jack. Not let him git away an' take him an' cut off his head jis like they had the twelve wise doctors that had give his daughter up to die. Jack didn't know what to do. So he bagged the King fer twenty-four hours time to go an' git his magic sack. Hit might save her he tol' him. So the ol' King said all right, he would give 'im twenty-four hours, but not a minute longer. So Jack he hit a runnin'. He run an' he run tell he got to his house an' got his magic sack an' then he run an' he run an' he run tell he got back to the King's house.

The King's daughter was very porely by that time. Jis could tell they'uz breath in 'er. So Jack he called fer some more clear spring water. This was his las' chance an' he knowed hit. So he got the water. Filled up his glass. Looked fust at the foot of the girl's bed. Thar'uz nothin' thar. Then he looked through the glass at the head of the bed an' thar stood Death reachin' out to grab the King's daughter. Oh, his ol' bony fingers was jes right down ready to take holt of her throat. Jack knowed he didn't have a minute to lose. So he drapped his glass an' grabbed his sack an' holdin' the mouth open with one hand he slapped on the side with the other an' said:

"Whickety whack,
Jump into my sack"

An' Death lef' the head of the girl's bed an' jumped into the sack an' Jack tied it up in thar an' throwed hit across his shoulder an' took hit home with him. The girl got well right then, an' the ol' King give Jack a bushel of gold.

So Jack had all the money he'd ever need an' he decided to

settle down an' stay at home. He never went out anywhere. When he wanted anything to eat he'd send his servants to town an' they'd hawl in a great supply. He didn't notice the passin' of time. Hit jis went on an' on an' Jack got so he didn't pay no 'tention to it. Fust thing he knowed he was old an' had a great long white beard, but he felt jis as young an' healthy as ever.

So one bright summer day Jack thought he'd walk to the nearest town an' see what everybody roun' thar was a-doin'. As he went along he noticed a sight of ol' people. All seemed to be awful ol' lookin' but they all seemed healthy an' acted as young as boys an' girls.

Goin' long down the road he met an' ol' ol' woman. She seemed to be in trouble bout somethin'. So Jack he stopped an' axed her. "Say, granny," he said, says he: "You seem to be in trouble. What's the matter? Looks like you'd a been dead with ol' age long ago." "That's jist hit," she tol' Jack. "That's hit. I ort to be dead long ago. I'm nearly two hundred years ol'. But didn't ye know. Some fool has got Death tied up in a sack somers an' nobody can die. I wish I could."

An' then for the fust time sence he'd put Death in his sack, Jack thought about it an' that he hadn't never turned him loose. An' jis to please the ol' woman that wanted to die he went back home an' untied the sack. Death jumped out an' right out o' the door he went. An' he went this way an' he went that way an' people died so fast that the livin' ones couldn't bury 'em. An' that night Jack felt weak an' sick hisse'f. He got up an' seed he couldn't hardly stan' on his feet. He'uz so tottery. He got his magic glass an' filled hit full of clear spring water an' helt hit up an' looked through hit an' thar stood Death at the head of his bed a-grinnin' at him. An' Jack was dead in his bed the next mornin'.

Collected by James Taylor Adams on October 21, 1941, from Gaines Kilgore at the Wise County Fairgrounds. This tale is a combination of Type 330, "The Smith Outwits the Devil," and Type 332, "Godfather Death." See Chase, Jack Tales, SOLDIER JACK.

ONCE THERE WAS A MAN who had three sons, Jack, Will and Tom. Tom and Will who was next oldest to Tom were several years older than Jack. Their old man thought as much of one as he did the other but as these two were older he wanted them to have a good education and make something out of themselves. He loved Jack too but it was not time for him to be sent away to school and he only awaited his time, then he too would have a chance to learn something and make his way in the world. The old man gave Tom and Will every thing on earth that was needed in the way of education, sent them to school, sent them money, clothes and other good things that every boy never had before. They'd write back and ask for money, saying they needed it for this and that, and, in the end the old man would wind up by sending it to them. He had sent them to one of the best colleges of that day and after several years he heard of one of them being sent to the Pen at Frankfort for stealing something. Later he got word that his other boy had turned out to be a thief also and he was in the Pen also near his brother. After some letters and investigation he was told that his boys had both turned out to be nothing but regular thieves. He learned that they would steal from stores and public buildings or anywhere else that anything was laying around loose. That they had been doing this all the time that he thought they had been learning an education and preparing themselves to step out into the world and make their own living. It is needless to say that the old man was very disheartened at this news and for some time he remained at home in a sorrowful mood. At last he saw that that would not get him anywhere and that he had one more son, Jack who he would do a job on that was to his notions. He had tried to raise his other two to make something he wanted them to, but they had made what they wanted to make themselves so he was determined to see that his boy made what he wanted him to this time and he made up his mind if his boys were to all make thieves that he would see to it that his last boy would make a damned good one if he had anything to do with it. He didn't want it said that he could not train his boys for what he wanted them to be. So, in time Jack was made ready to be sent away to train for the future and he got in touch with some tough bandits and old-time gangsters in Louisville and Lexington where crime was at that time rampant. It was not long, however until he had made connections with the proper ones or to his liking and he sent Jack to them telling him to do as they told him at all times and to see what a good mark he could make at thieving. In time Jack met the parties and at once was sent on a life of crime which mostly meant a stealing job. The men were glad to get him for their jobs and trained him to perfection, if that can be said of such work. All in all he made a good thief as far as his teachers were concerned.

The old man kept in touch with the gangsters and they informed him that his son was doing a splendid job with them and would be able to take care of himself soon. In fact they had used him until they thought it might be best to get rid of him before he knew too much. So they wrote to the old man and told him they were sending him home soon. The old man wrote his thanks with the money for pay for his training saying, "I don't want no one-horse rogue in the family, if they gotta be thieves they'll have to be goddam good ones."

The boy arrived one evening just about dark and after greeting the old man and the sisters and mother they sat down to a good old country-meal. At the table the old man inquired as to what kind of thief he thought he could make in the future. "Well," said Jack, "I don't know what you think about it. I can steal the very sheet off your bed and you sleeping in it," and he went about eating his supper as if he had said nothing unusual. The old man eyed the son across the table with a doubtful look and made fun of him, saying, "I don't believe any of that stuff son, no one could pull that over me."

They lived in an old log house back in the foothills of Kentucky and a good many years had seasoned it out good in every way. It had the old fire place, the ladder leading up to the loft and the punchin' floors that most all of the cabins were made with in the early days. The punchin' boards are cut with a fro and hewn down on the sides so they will fit close together to the ones on either side. The edges are made in a bevel-sort of way so that when they are placed on the floor they will fit even and stay there without moving about. The end boards are against a post or the wall and these two end boards hold all the others steady. When necessary you could lift any board you wanted up and replace it as easy. That was the kind of floor the old man had in his log cabin where he had raised his family and where the three brothers were all born. So as they finished the supper the boy told his old man to go on to bed with the rest of the family as usual and he would sit the night out on the front porch as he was eager to get some good cool, fresh, country air. The old man started to go to bed but the son, Jack, reminded him to bar the door as he had always done before. After doing this the old man retired to his bed and was soon fast asleep.

Jack waited a while and then stole underneath the floor of the bedroom where his old man slept and raised one of the punchin's up and crawled up into the room near the bed where the old man lay snoring. The old man was a restless sleeper and every time he would move or turn over in the bed, Jack who had taken hold of the edge of the sheet would pull it out from under him inch by inch. It was a long and nerve racking job but he finally got it out from underneath him and rolled it up under his arm. He then went back down through the hole where he had crawled in and laid the punchin' in its place as it had been before. He hid the sheet in the smoke-house and returned to a big home-made chair on the porch where he curled up and was soon fast asleep himself, dreaming of the city where he had been for the past year or so.

Morning came and the old man made the fires and opened the door. Jack awoke and went into the house. The old lady started breakfast and soon they were at the table eating breakfast. The old man started bantering Jack about his braggin' about the sheet stealing and Jack just sat in silence until he had eated his meal. Then he told him to see where his sheet was off his bed. The old man went to the bed and saw his sheet gone.

Jack told him to go to a place in the wood shed and there he found the sheet. He had made a good thief.

Collected by James M. Hylton on March 9, 1942, from Fugate Bryant, aged about 43 years. Bryant was a coal miner near Wise, Virginia. He had known the tale all his life, having heard it many times from his parents. Type 1525, "The Master Thief."

19 / *How Jack Got Tom To Do Will's Hard Work*

JACK AND TOM AND WILL was all brothers and liked to go huntin' and fishin' down on the river but for some reasons known to themselves Jack and Will wanted to go theirselves on this trip I'm telling you about and they had to figure some way for to get away from him and yet they had been told by their Pap to get that big pile of wood moved from out on the section to the shed at the barn place and today was the time to do it and when their Pap said today was the time he meant within that day and before darkness fell too. Tom had a wheelbarrow he'd made from some fine new strips from a stove crate and he's a bit proud of it and was always trying to show it off to everybody. Well, Jack winked at Will an' told him to say nuthin' which he didn't an' he went to the wheelbarrow an' looked down at it an' said to Tom, "Tom, I don't believe that a wheelbarrow like this will stand up to any long haulin' an' if it would it is a good 'un. I heard Will say that it wasn't no good anyhow an' he didn't think it'd haul much at a time an' all that stuff. I'm startin' to think the same myself too. We figure it'd hold up a load or trip or two but not fer long." It made Tom splutter an' move about an' he told them to show him the thing that it wouldn't haul. Whereupon Jack said he couldn't haul the wood to the shed and he went off to get the barrow an' said, he'd show 'em. Well, they left an' was gone all day laughin' how Tom had hauled the wood an' here they was on a river bank fishin' an' havin' a good time. But Tom's Pap showed up a little while after

Ina Purkey Carter and Claude Richard Carter. Mr. Carter told "How Jack Got Tom to Do Will's Hard Work" (No. 19). Photo courtesy of the Carters' daughter, Mrs. Anita C. Healy.

they'd left an' when he saw the trick they'd played on him he and Tom had a few words together an' waited on Jack and Will to come home. When they did, Pap told them that Tom had been such a good boy haulin' the wood he was goin' to take him on a weeks fishin' trip with him an' that Jack an' Will would have to take care of the place an' do all the chores around the place. They liked to killed theirselves the next week workin' then Pap told them he had give up the idea as it was too late in the season, an' Tom got a laugh.

Collected by James M. Hylton on August 27, 1941, from Claude Carter aged 33 years. Claude is a son of Owen C. Carter, Deputy Sheriff of Wise County. Claude was raised in Wise County but had traveled around a bit as a young man and had heard this tale from a German rancher in Colorado.

This old general store in Pound (Wise Co.), Virginia was used by the WPA to house a weaving project. Va. Neg. 19094, November 1938, Record Group 69-N, Box 105, Virginia-Washington, General Subject Series, 1933-44, Still Photographs, National Archives.

The Pound weaving project. Woman seated is spinning wool; the woman standing is operating a cracker reeling machine. Va. Neg. 19107, November 1938, Record Group 69-N, Box 105, Virginia-Washington, General Subject Series, 1933-44, Still Photographs, National Archives.

Pupils of the Big Stone Gap (Wise Co.) School are taught ceramics as part of their regular school studies by the Federal Art Project. Va. Neg. 19116, November 1938, Record Group 69-N, Box 105, Virginia-Washington, General Subject Series, 1933-44, Still Photographs, National Archives.

"The Village Smithy," a diorama made by James E. True, an artist on the Virginia Art Project. This diorama, along with six others, is housed in the Southwest Virginia Museum in Big Stone Gap. Photo by Charles L. Perdue, Jr.

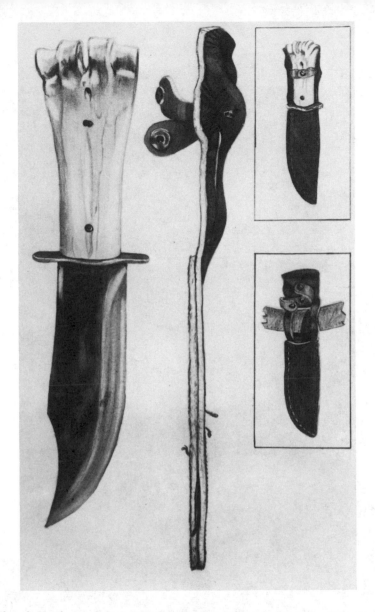

Sheath Knife. Made by Leonard C. Freeman of Dryden, Lee Co., VA, about 1886. "The blade was ground from an old crosscut saw and the handle fashioned from the shin bone of a young calf." The sheath for the knife was made "from an old set of harness and probably at a much later date." This item "was donated to the Janie Slemp Newman Memorial Collection [now the Southwest Virginia Museum, Big Stone Gap, VA] by the maker through Campbell Slemp, grandson of the late Campbell Slemp, former member of Congress and colonel of the 64th Regiment Virginia Infantry, C.S.A. This item was documented in 1936 by artist Jess W. Skeen. Recent research indicates that this item is not in the collection of the Southwest Virginia Museum at the present time. Index of American Design (VA-me-1); National Gallery of Art, Washington.

Powell Valley. Photo by Burchette's Studio, from Luther F. Addington, The Story of Wise County (Virginia), *and used with permission of Mrs. Luther F. Addington.*

Samuel Salyers, builder of the second house in Norton and father of Civil War Col. Logan Salyers. Photo from Luther F. Addington, The Story of Wise County (Virginia), *and used with permission of Mrs. Luther F. Addington.*

The Bruce House near Coeburn. Photo from Luther F. Addington, The Story of Wise County (Virginia), *and used with permission of Mrs. Luther F. Addington.*

Volley Stidham and his wife Myrtle at one of the looms constructed by Mr. Stidham for the WPA weaving project in Pound (Wise County), Virginia. Va. Neg. 19108, November 1938, Record Group 69-N, Box 105, Virginia-Washington, General Subject Series, 1933-44, Still Photographs, National Archives.

Six generations on the ninety-ninth birthday of Delilah Hubbard. From left: Ted Adams, Lona Adams, Savannah Childers, Sarah Jane Mullins, Mary Hubbard, and Delilah Hubbard. Photo from Luther F. Addinton, The Story of Wise County (Virginia), and used with permission of Mrs. Luther F. Addington.

The Riverside Hotel, St. Paul, in 1901. Photo from Luther F. Addington, The Story of Wise County (Virginia), and used with permission of Mrs. Luther F. Addington.

Dwina schoolhouse, built about 1870. Photo courtesy Dr. J.N. Hillman, who attended the school, from Luther F. Addington, The Story of Wise County (Virginia), and used with permission of Mrs. Luther F. Addington.

Mrs. Mahaley Bradley and her big spinning wheel. Photo from Luther F. Addington, The Story of Wise County (Virginia), and used with permission of Mrs. Luther F. Addington.

Dicy Roberts Adams (1893-1983), wife of James Taylor Adams, in 1980. Mrs. Adams was a prolific informant who contributed dozens of tales, songs, and other items of folklore to the Virginia Writers' Project. Photo courtesy Mrs. Adams' great grandson, Fletcher Dean.

Lenore Corene Kilgore, daughter of James Taylor Adams. She told "Jack Goes to Seek His Fortune" (No. 11). Photo courtesy of Mrs. Kilgore's sister, Mrs. Naomi Adams Mullins.

Spencer Adams, son of James Taylor Adams, standing at his father's grave in Big Laurel on Fathers' Day, 1985. He told "Jack and the Woodchopper" (No. 14). Photo courtesy of Mr. Adams's sister, Mrs. Naomi Adams Mullins.

89

James Taylor Adams (1892-1954). Photo from Virginia Caval-
cade, *VOl. 21, No. 4, Spring 1972.*

Old Jack
and the New Deal

THE VIRGINIA WRITERS' PROJECT AND JACK
TALE COLLECTING IN WISE COUNTY, VIRGINIA

WHEN RICHARD CHASES'S *THE JACK TALES* was published in 1943 it was generally well received and well reviewed. Joseph M. Carriere of the University of Virginia reviewed it for the *Journal of American Folklore* (January-March, 1946), and he stated that the book was "a major contribution to the field of the Anglo-American folktale." *The Jack Tales* became, as Leondard Roberts was to put it later, "an American folktale classic,"[2] and some writers have acclaimed Chase as "an internationally known folklorist."[3] Despite the reservations of some scholars regarding Chase's methods, *The Jack Tales* has become, in effect and in practice, the standard work in this narrowly defined area of folktale scholarship and it is representative of the work done in a certain period in the development of folklore scholarship. As an academic folklorist, I am necessarily interested in these aspects of the history of the discipline.

This article and my concern with Richard Chase and Jack tales, specifically, grew out of my longstanding interest in the

New Deal programs in Virginia and their involvement with folk culture in many different areas, a subject on which my wife, Nancy Martin-Perdue, and I have been conducting research over the past several years. This recent work overlaps and is directly connected in a complex network of interrelationships with our prior work on the people displaced by the creation of Shenandoah National Park. In pursuit of these combined projects, we unforeseeably uncovered information on Richard Chase's use of Jack tales and other material from Virginia—a use which has only been briefly alluded to in occasional citations and the details of which have been generally unknown or unavailable.

In addition, the material thus turned up in the course of our work finally provides the possibility for comparative analysis between the manuscript texts accompanying this article and some of the Jack tales that have been edited, collated, abridged, and changed, and presented to the public by Richard Chase in his books. While scholars have long known of the editing practices which Chase, himself, readily admitted to, it has been impossible to judge the extent to which he carried on such activities due to the lack of original materials—a fact which contributed heavily to the reservations expressed by many scholars about Chase's work.

As an academic folklorist, I am interested in change, as well as tradition, for change represents the dynamic face of traditional folklore expression. But as a folklore scholar, I am necessarily more concerned with change which occurs in the normal context of the traditional folklore performance, rather than in change imposed from outside that context. In other words, changes made by Gaines Kilgore in repeated performances of telling the same Jack tale which he had learned from his grandfather are *not* equivalent to conscious decisions made by Richard Chase to add motifs from European sources or to delete material based on his own outside and elite aesthetic or intuitions. In my role as folklorist my primary concern is with the cultural materials resulting from the former situation and with locating, recording, and preserving those materials in a form as close as possible to that which the informant originally used. At the same time, folklorists cannot afford to ignore the effects of

Master Storyteller
RICHARD CHASE

Scheduling brochure distributed by Richard Chase from Huntsville, Alabama, n.d.

RICHARD CHASE
FOLKLORIST
&
MASTER STORYTELLER
Compiler of
THE JACK TALES
GRANDFATHER TALES

93

change of the latter sort upon the material and people which we ordinarily study.

Finally, using the broader perspective of our other research and concerns with ethnicity and identity, cultural geography and dislocation, kinship and local history, I am able to provide specific details and a context for Chase's work in Virginia. This background also allows us to assess his role appropriately as one of many outside agents in an extensive web of actors operating to bring about a process of vast social change, on the one hand, and as a self-serving, self-aggrandizing individual exploiting opportunities provided to him by various agencies, on the other.

In addition to the questions relating to folklore scholarship mentioned earlier, there are a number of larger concerns and issues which are implicit in this case—most of which are far too complex and far-reaching to be considered in depth here, but which call to mind such treatments as David Whisnant's consideration of "the politics of culture" in *All That Is Native and Fine*. Discussions of such issues need to be kept in mind throughout this presentation for they are relevant to the case even though the points may not be made explicit here.

First and foremost, there are underlying themes in this case of internal colonialism, operating by way of direct State involvement in and manipulation of traditional culture through the agency of the Virginia Writers' Project. There are also obvious overtones of regional stereotyping, of class distinctions, and socioeconomic differences which affect relationships and are expressed in various ways throughout the material.

And since Chase was never content to merely collect folklore, but was likewise actively engaged in performing and interpreting folklore materials for much wider audiences, there are the problematic ethical questions posed by the appropriation and performance of some aspect of another group or sub-group's culture. To a great extent, culture *is* identity. When an outsider says by his or her words and/or actions, "I like this part of your identity but I can improve upon it and I can perform it, i.e., represent you and that part of your expressive culture, better than you can," the potential results of such performance are both multiple and complex, affecting both the individual and his/her community.

Often the group from which the material is obtained finds its cultural identity compromised, stereotyped, or otherwise misrepresented in the interchange and the outside individual or group enriched at its expense in the process. But an outsider's attention may foster a local revival of interest in certain cultural practices; some members of the sub-group may enjoy the "validation" implied by the interest of the larger society; or some individuals may perceive that they are being exploited but do not feel that there is anything which can be done about it because of their position as members of the sub-group or because of other contraints, such as needs for employment. To some extent all of these things occurred in Wise County viz-a-viz Richard Chase and the Virginia Writers' Project folklore collecting program.

Traditional culture, wherever it might be found, has generally been treated by dominant groups of the larger society as a resource to be exploited. Workers on many of the New Deal cultural programs accepted such views as that expressed by Cecil Sharp and espoused by Richard Chase and others, that the local or indigenous culture of Appalachia was, in effect, the "racial inheritance" of all American people—regardless of their actual cultural diversity, history, and experience. From this ideological position, they could easily maintain that traditional, localized cultural material should serve as a resource out of which to produce a National Art, Literature, or Music. From this ideological position also, some individuals—Chase included—could and did use the opportunity and the system to further their own individual ends.

But we do not easily tolerate such cultural exploitation in other areas of the larger society. We protect our territories with boundaries and treaties and our cultural productions with copyrights. If someone borrows an elite cultural artistic product, changes it, and publishes or performs it, we can sue the guilty party and demand a fair share of the proceeds realized from its performance. Equal protection has not been generally extended to traditional culture or its bearers.

The question of copyright of cultural products is not brought up here lightly. There has been, in fact, a serious movement in this direction, with a conference held in Geneva, Switzerland several years ago and attended by Alan Jabbour as representative of the American Folklife Center. The conference was sponsored largely by Third-World nations in order to consider ways of copyrighting and protecting their rights to their own cultural traditions and expressions. The whole concept is fraught with incredible difficulties of definition and enforcement and I, for one, am not advocating copyrighting folklore. However, again in my role as an academic folklorist, it is incumbent upon me to be aware of and to consider such movements and to weigh the possible impact of such ideas upon my own personal areas of concern and work. Copyright laws would doubtless not hinder the infringement of cultural "rights" as exhibited in this case, just as Prohibition did not stop the production of whiskey. And in fact such laws, if enacted, could ultimately have unintentional adverse effects upon traditional culture by institutionalizing it and turning it into a consciously produced commodity. We need other ways of dealing with such intractable problems but it is not yet clear what they might be. Perhaps all we can do is see that these issues are brought up for public awareness and discussion.

Following, I will give a very brief overview of the historical references to Jack tales as they occur in some of the literature. Then I will proceed to a descriptive account and presentation of data which sheds light on the role of Richard Chase in the collection of Jack tales and other folklore in Wise County, Virginia, as well as information on the ultimately more important role played by Wise County native, James Taylor Adams, in that same endeavor. The collecting project which involved both Chase and Adams was sponsored and funded by the Virginia Writers' Project of the Work Projects Administration in 1941-42.

* * *

There is enough evidence available to document the existence of a long-lived and once fairly extensive Jack tale tradition in the

United States, dating back to before the Revolutionary War. Some early evidence for this tradition is provided by the Rev. Dr. Joseph Doddridge in his notes published in 1824 on frontier life in western Pennsylvania and Virginia (now West Virginia) between 1763 and 1783:

Dramatic narrations, chiefly concerning Jack and the Giant, furnished our young people with another source of amusement during their leisure hours. Many of those tales were lengthy, and embraced a considerable range of incident. Jack, always the hero of the story, after encountering many difficulties, and performing many great achievements, came off conqueror of the Giant. Many of these stories were tales of knight-errantry, in which case some captive virgin was released from captivity and restored to her lover. These dramatic narrations concerning Jack and the Giant bore a strong resemblance to the poems of Ossian, the story of the Cyclops and Ulysses in the Odyssey of Homer, and the tale of the Giant and Great-heart in the Pilgrim's Progress, and were so arranged as to the different incidents of the narration, that they were easily committed to memory. They certainly have been handed down from generation to generation from time immemorial. Civilization has indeed banished the use of those ancient tales of romantic heroism; but what then? It has substituted in their place the novel and romance.[4]

In 1888, in the very first volume of the *Journal of American Folklore*, William Wells Newell presented two Jack tales that were in oral tradition in the mid-1800s in Ohio and Massachusetts (versions of Type 130, "The Animals in Night Quarters"). An article by Isabel Gordon Carter, published in the *Journal of American Folklore* in 1925 (June-September) contained 11 Jack tales collected from Jane Gentry of western North Carolina. The source of Gentry's tales was her grandfather, Council Harmon. Harmon was born in 1802 and died in 1896. His descendants— as well as others—kept the Jack tale tradition alive well into the twentieth century. Ultimately it was these Council Harmon descendants who were the source of the Jack tales collected in Beech Creek, North Carolina by Richard Chase.

Chase, himself, will readily tell those who ask that he was a brilliant child, pampered by a black nurse and rebellious

toward his dominating father's demand for discipline and sub-
mission to hard physical labor, and that he was soon sent away
to a special school for problem boys. By all accounts, including
my own observations made during several contacts with Chase
between 1956 and 1984, he is a shrewd, difficult, and erratic man
with a sizeable ego. For much of his life his ego has been well
served through his performances of songs, dances, tales, and
Punch and Judy shows, and through publications and public lectures. Chase can be quite personable and charming, and this has
enabled him time and again to convince others of his abilities
as a folklore collector and scholar. At the same time, he exhibits
a considerable ambivalence toward the role of scholar, and alter-
nates between proclaiming an extreme disdain for and arrogance
toward all academics and their inherent capabilities and express-
ing the hope of eventually finding a permanent position as
scholar-in-residence at some college or university.[5]

Chase indicated an ambivalence, as well, regarding his position viz-a-viz the "folk." He often included himself in an "us"
when he talked or wrote about the Wise County natives or
Southern Appalachian peoples in general. Sometimes he
expanded the definition of "folk" to be all-inclusive, writing,
". . . if each of us is not a member of that collectivity that is THE
FOLK what'n'ell are we?!" But, at the same time, he referred to
some of the Wise County people as "real folk" and seemed to
exclude himself from that category.[6]

Whatever else Chase was, he was clearly not "of the folk."
His family was from New England but his father established a
nursery near Huntsville, Alabama and that is where Richard
grew up.[7] At the age of 20, in 1924, he was in Boston where he
learned about the Pine Mountain Settlement School in Kentucky. He hitchhiked to the school where he heard the students
singing ballads and, as he put it, "My hair stood on end to hear
this thing happening." Chase seems to have undergone what
might best be described as a conversion experience. He learned
about the work of Cecil Sharp at Pine Mountain School and he
took as scripture a portion of the introduction to the 1917 edi-

tion of *English Folk Songs from the Southern Appalachians*. Sharp said,

> . . . remembering that the primary purpose of education is to place the children of the present generation in possession of the cultural achievements of the past, so that they may as quickly as possible enter into their racial inheritance, what better form of music or of literature can we give them than the folk-songs and folk-ballads of the race to which they belong, or of the nation whose language they speak? To deny them these is to cut them off from the past and to rob them of that which is theirs by right of birth.[8]

By his 21st birthday Chase was teaching songs from Sharp's collection to rural North Alabama school children, some of whom soon made Chase aware that there was still a living tradition of folksong in the area.

In the mid-1920s Chase attended Harvard for two years and he also took courses in progressive education with Marietta Johnson in Greenwich, Connecticut and Fair Hope, Alabama.[9] During this period he worked off and on in the field of recreation and as a performer/teacher of folksongs and dances. In 1929 he graduated from Antioch College with a B.S. in Botany. He had met his future wife at Antioch and in 1930 they were married and they spent the following two or three years in Europe—primarily in Switzerland and England, where he developed contacts with the English Folk Dance and Song Society.

In 1934 and apparently through most of 1936 Chase served as Associate Director of the Institute of Folk Music at the University of North Carolina in Chapel Hill. The Institute had been founded in September, 1931 for "the purpose of developing creative music distinctly American." This was to be done by "discovering, collecting, and studying native folk-music" and "encouraging creative composition based on this music," but the Institute's two major accomplishments were the establishment of the Dogwood Festival and the North Carolina Symphony Orchestra.[10] During this period Chase became involved with the White Top Folk Festival in Southwest Virginia, beginning work with the Festival in 1934 and remaining with it until its demise in 1941.[11]

In the Spring of 1935 Chase was hired to teach folksongs at a teachers' conference sponsored by the Office of Emergency Relief in Education. The conference was held in Raleigh, North Carolina and one of the attendees was Marshall Ward. Ward told Chase about his family in Beech Creek, North Carolina and about their Jack tales. This was Chase's first exposure to the existence of the Jack tales and he was excited at the prospect of uncovering an active tale-telling tradition in the North Carolina mountains. From that point on he focussed a great deal of his time and energy on the pursuit of Jack tales. He visited the Ward family in Beech Creek, collected their tales, and published six of them in the *Southern Folklore Quarterly* beginning with Volume I, Number I, 1937, and continuing into 1941.[12]

In 1937 Chase moved to Richmond, Virginia where he worked for the WPA's Recreation Division and also served as the Virginia Representative of the English Folk Dance and Song Society of America. In March of 1939, while still living in Richmond, Chase met Herbert Halpert who was just beginning his Southern recording expedition for the WPA's Joint Committee on the Folk Arts. Chase was looking for a way to obtain enough money to complete his work on the Jack tales and publish a book on them. He had earlier talked to Benjamin Botkin in the Washington office of the Federal Writers' Project about his proposed Jack tale work but decided after conversations with Halpert to submit a proposal through the Recreation Division and the Joint Committee on the Folk Arts.

Chase wrote on March 19, 1939 to Nicholas Ray, Drama Consultant for the Recreation Division, stating: "The people who know these tales are all in North Carolina, and I understand that such a project cannot be set up under the W.P.A. of Virginia."[13]

Nicholas Ray was favorably impressed with Chase and his project and wanted to expand it to include folklore collectors in other states, specifically mentioning Arkansas. Unfortunately for Chase the proposal was made at a time when the WPA cultural programs were going through a period of retrenchment and re-organization, and he was unable to get it funded.[14]

By mid-March, 1940 Chase had moved to Glade Spring, Virginia (Washington County)—apparently to be closer to the site of the White Top Festival. Here he began a correspondence with James Taylor Adams of Big Laurel, Wise County, Virginia. Adams was a local man, Postmaster of Big Laurel, a writer, and sometime publisher of short-lived literary magazines. He had been interested in folklore all his life and had begun collecting traditional songs and tales in Wise and adjoining counties in Virginia and Kentucky about 1925. He began working with the WPA in 1936, documenting local history and artifacts for the Virginia Historic Inventories Project. In March of 1938 he transferred to the Virginia Writers' Project and by the time that project was terminated he had collected more than twice as much folklore and song material as any other Project worker in Virginia. We will give more consideration to Adams' background at a later point in this article.[15]

Chase and Adams's initial correspondence had to do with collecting ballads and with the possibility of Adams bringing performers to the White Top Festival planned for August 1940—but cancelled due to rain and local flooding. In October 1940 Chase visited the Ward family in Beech Creek and while there learned that Adams had sent the Wards some folklore material including at least one Jack tale ("JACK AND THE BULL"). Chase wrote to Adams on October 25 asking for permission to include "JACK AND THE BULL" in his planned book of Jack tales. He also inquired as to whether or not Adams had run across any more Jack tales.[16]

No correspondence seems to have survived from the following nine months but in September, 1941 Chase wrote to Adams about a proposed book on Wise County folklore to be prepared and published under the auspices of the Virginia Writers' Project. Since Chase had been trying for some time to find a way to fund his Jack tale book project, and in the absence of any evidence to the contrary, we can only infer that the proposal for a Wise County folklore book was instigated by him, following up on his correspondence with James Taylor Adams and his examination of the Wise County material in the Virginia Writers' Project files in Richmond. He enclosed an outline he had drawn up which indicated that the book would make use of "all genuine folk lore of value to the intrinsic purposes of the general scheme," and some of the types of folklore he listed were: songs, ballads, carols, fiddle tunes, hymns, birth lore, marriage lore, death lore, crafts, play-parties, dances, and tales. James Taylor Adams and James Hylton of Wise County were to do interviewing and collecting of appropriate material; Chase was to do arranging of material (that is, collating versions of stories and songs) and preliminary editing; the Richmond office staff of the Virginia Writers' Project was to do final editing of the book. Chase may not have worked full time for the Writers' Project but he did receive several allowances for travel in order to do field collecting in Wise County.[17]

Chase spent four days in Wise County in early October and on his return home wrote to Eudora Ramsay Richardson, Director of the Virginia Writers' Project that the Wise County folklore book should focus entirely on tales rather than folklore generally. This was, in fact, James Taylor Adams's suggestion to Chase but Chase neglected to mention this in his letter.[18]

From the beginning there was conflict between the field workers, on the one hand, and Chase and the Richmond office, on the other, over the way the tales were to be edited. Adams wrote to Richardson that the proposed book was not what he expected and he told her:

[Chase's] idea is to take the tales we have collected in Wise County and rewrite them, making them into more readable stories, adding touches of completeness so that they will appear as found in 16th and 17th century collections, while mine would have been to record and preserve these tales exactly, as far as possible, as we took them down from the tellers.[19]

Adams was soon set straight by a letter from Miriam Sizer, Folklore Consultant with the Virginia Writers' Project in Richmond. She first complemented Adams on his good work (as she did in every letter to a field worker) and then went on to say:

The work of the collector is to take down the 'lore' exactly as the informant gives it. It is only upon such authentic data that the incidents, speech, history, and atmosphere of folklore can be preserved. The editor or writer of folklore, especially prose materials, has a slightly different problem. He looks at the story from the reader's point of view. For instance, take 'Jack and the Bull.' The several variants contain different incidents of adventure. It makes a much better story to combine all the incidents into one story than to have several separate similar stories. All the elements of folklore are kept intact, while variety of incident deepens interest and enriches the scope of the tale. The composite story actually gives a truer picture of the whole story than any one variant. But unless the variants are genuine the composite is a sham. All the variants of a given folk tale, ballad, or folk song make up the cycle of that folklore unit. Any given variant is just as authentic as any other. One variant may be rare and more valuable than another; but each one contributes to and is included in the cycle. As long as songs, stories, and any other lore remain in oral tradition, their cycles are incomplete.[20]

Chase and Sizer were in total agreement on the matter— it is alright to rewrite folklore but you want to be sure you are rewriting authentic material. I should point out here that the notion of folk cultural material as a wellspring of inspiration for, or a resource for exploitation by, writers, artists, scholars, and others was (and is) a common one. For example, the Index of American Design, another WPA program in the 1930s, proceeded in its "pictorial survey of design in the American decorative, useful and folk arts," with the main purpose of making available "usable source records of this material to artists, designers, manufacturers, museums, libraries, and art schools."[21]

Between October 1941 and March 1942 Chase spent several weeks in Wise County, working usually with James Taylor Adams or James Hylton but sometimes working alone. He was also given considerable material from the Writers' Project files in Richmond. The Richmond Office was supposed to retain duplicates of any material given to Chase but, in many cases, gave him the original material and kept no duplicates.

In March, 1942 Chase moved to Proffit, Virginia (Albemarle County) and correspondence between him and Adams regarding the proposed Wise County book continued from that address until the Writers' Project closed down in mid-June of 1942. After that there were a few references to the material gathered for the book and several statements from Chase to Adams on the possibility of getting it together, but the book effectively died with the close of the Writers' Project.

When we interviewed Richard Chase in Alabama in November of 1984 he said that he did not remember anything about working with the Writers' Project or about any proposed Wise County folklore book. Nonetheless, there are extant several draft versions of outlines, lists of tales and other items to be included in the book, and an occasional page or two of introductory material—all written by Chase.[22] Chase also did not remember taking any file material from the VWP office in Richmond but his statements in correspondence indicate otherwise:

I was in Richmond a week ago, and brought home a big batch of the folklore materials gathered by you [Adams] and your co-workers Emory Hamilton and James Hylton.[23] . . .Your Gaines Kilgore's "Willie and the Devil" is sure a honey![24]

And a letter from Miriam Sizer to James Taylor Adams acknowledges the fact that Adams's material was reaching the Richmond office:

Your prose materials are interesting, especially the folktales. They seem to be good variants of the Jack tales.[25]

When the Virginia Writers' Project closed and the folklore collection was deposited in Alderman Library at the University of Virginia the original manuscript copy of WILLIE AND THE DEVIL was missing, along with several hundred other tales, songs, and miscellaneous items of Wise County folklore. According to Chase most of the material in his possession burned up in a house fire in Beech Creek, North Carolina. We are indebted to James Taylor Adams for his foresight in retaining copies of material he sent to Richmond, and we are indebted to the Adams family, and to Helen Lewis and Emory Hamilton for seeing that the Adams Papers were preserved—at first archived in the Manuscripts Department of Alderman Library, University of Virginia and later transferred to the James Cook Wyllie Library, Clinch Valley College, Wise, Virginia.

It is not surprising that James Taylor Adams and his family were interested in preserving the traditional culture of Wise County. It was, after all, their own.[26] The Adams's ancestors had been in the Wise County area since 1810 when they arrived from Western North Carolina. James Taylor Adams was well qualified to talk about traditions in his part of Virginia:

My father, Joseph Adams, died when I was eight, but even before his death, my most pleasant memories are of the long winter evenings when I sat spellbound at his feet or at the feet of my mother and listened as they told me tales about boys named Jack who went to seek their fortune, or of giants who carried little boys off to their caves and eat them.[27]

Adams goes on to discuss at length the various forms of folklore he remembers from his youth, as well as the beliefs, crafts, and other aspects of folklife in earlier times in Wise. Several members of his family had had personal experiences with witchcraft; his grandfather was an herb doctor; and most of his family and their neighbors sang, told tales, and attended dances regularly. It was, says Adams, "an atmosphere of almost constant singing and tale telling. There were no other forms of amusement and entertainment in that day."[28]

Adams was born in 1892—at the very beginning of the coal and timber boom that would last into the 1920s, bringing a huge increase in population and economic changes that would contribute to eliminating the lifestyle that Adams spent so much time in documenting. The population of Wise County increased from 19,652 in 1900 to 45,721 in 1920. The boom was over in the mid-1920s and by 1935 one-fifth of Wise County's population was on relief—the highest percentage of any county in Vir-

James Taylor Adams, ca. 1936. Cover photo, Frederic D. Vanover, James Taylor Adams, Mountain Poet Historian: A Brief Biography *(Louisville: Dixieana Press, 1937).*

ginia. And in 1934 and 1935 more relief money went into Wise than any other county—three times as much as the next highest county.[29] It is perhaps appropriate that Wise County contributed more than half of all the folklore and folksongs collected by the Writers' Project in Virginia.

Adams knew that he was conducting a salvage operation and he says:

Folk tales have almost been forgotten, but there are still a few old timers. . .who like to tell the old tales to an audience wherever it may be had.[30]

But he also admitted:

I have been most successful with people of middle age, say from thirty to sixty-five. As a rule people under thirty are not interested in folk lore and people above seventy-five have poor memory or they have lost all interest in life and it is difficult to get them to talk on any subject other than one of their own chosing[sic].[31]

Adams notes a small revival of one type of folklore which was brought about by the Federal Writers' Project's efforts to document it:

The folk dances and folk plays had become almost lost to the present generation. But during the last year there has been a revival of both the games and dances among the younger set. This was brought about by Federal Writers' Project workers searching for these old plays and dances. Just as the "Big Apple" was in full swing, in stepped a research worker asking if anyone present knew how to play "Skip-to-my Lou" or "Boston." No one knew, but they asked their parents who referred them to grandpap and granny who remembered the plays and dances and were, in most cases glad of the opportunity to teach their grandchildren how to do them, so the result is there is a revival going on in the Cumberlands and young men and women are swinging to the tunes, dances and playing games that their fathers and mothers never knew, and their grandfathers and grandmothers had almost forgotten.[32]

It seems likely that this is much more common than discussions in the literature might indicate and that such a revival accounts, in part, for the tremendous volume of songs, tales, and other lore turned in by the three Wise County workers.

Adams did not own a car and almost all of the material he turned in he had collected on foot, sometimes staying over wherever night happened to catch him. But when Richard Chase made his several visits to the County he came in his car and Adams then had the opportunity to tap new resources:

We drove up the Mullins Fork of Bold Camp as far [as] we could find a road and got out of the car and walked about five hundred yards through a snow storm along a winding, upward trail, to Emory Thacker's where we met Nancy (Old Granny) Shores. We did not know much about Granny's ability as a tale teller, but acted on a hunch. But we were pleasantly surprised for we had no more than got seated until the old lady, politely refusing a medicated cigarette which Dick offered her, reached into her waist-hung pocket and fished out a half-used twist of greenish and strong-smelling homemade tobacco and began whittling it off and cramming it into the bowl of an old clay pipe with a reed stem. All the time she was answering our questions about her early life and her experience as a midwife. . . .Then we got around to the subject of folk songs and tales. Granny said she used to *sing a sight*, but her voice was gone and she couldn't carry a tune any more. But she could tell tales and she had only last night told Emory's children that one about "Jack and his bull." She said she knowed a lot of tales, but she just couldn't think of them right then. "Did ye ever hear that one about Jack and old King Morock?" she asked. We told [her] we had not and she went on. "Well I'll tell hit to you. Hit'll take me an hour, but hit shore is a good tale. I think hit is." And, refilling her pipe and lighting it with a splinter held to the side of the red hot stove, she began . . .[33]

Adams elaborates further on his tale collecting methodology:

I have found that the best way to get the ordinary taleteller started off is to talk about other things at first, then gradually drift around to old times and old tales. I usually tell one myself, chosing one of the shorter ones like "The Big Toe," or "Fat and Lean," anything which I think might stir the memory of my prospective informant. Then I refer to my "finder list" (on the sly if possible) and go over the titles and list characters. If he knows a tale this usually reminds him of it.

I have found that the term "old tale" confuses the average person. They will start off by telling a hunting tale or some other local happening. And "traditional tale" means nothing whatever. The only way I have been able to explain what I am looking for is to tell one of the tales myself. My experience [has been] that no two people, even though members of the same family, will tell a tale in the same way. The fact is, the same person will tell the same tale differently every time they tell it. I have found that it is best to record the telling, then go back a second and sometimes a third time and hear it retold. This can be handled without exciting suspicion by taking along another party each time who never heard the tale. I have recorded one tale three times from the same informant. All were different. In one telling one part of the tale was left out entirely, and another character was introduced.[34]

In 1941, in addition to having actively worked as a folklore collector for some sixteen years, Adams was a writer of considerable experience. His best known work is probably *Death in the Dark: A Collection of Factual Ballads of American Mine Disasters, with Historical Notes*, but he was also a local correspondent for a number of newspapers and he had published numerous articles in magazines and newspapers—in addition to publishing magazines of his own. He used folklore and local history in much of his writing but, unlike Chase, he seems clearly to have distinguished between documenting folklore and using it for literary purposes. For example, he used JACK'S GOOSE (No. 15 in this article) in a story called "Jack's Goose." He added a seven-page literary setting and had his grandfather, Spencer Adams, tell an eighteen-page version of the tale of JACK'S GOOSE— but the story was not presented as collected folklore.[35]

Adams devised several literary frameworks for his stories: "Picked Up in Passing," "Appalachian Tales," and "Grandpap Told Me Tales." He also wrote factual "detective stories" based on songs and tales about historical events such as the ballad "Poor Ellen Smith," and he had some of these published.[36]

One-third of the Jack tales collected in Wise County—as well as dozens of others items of folklore—came from members of the Adams family. But James Taylor Adams moved in two worlds. He was "of the folk" and, yet, he was knowledgeable and sophisticated in regard to folklore. Adams had a keen interest in local history and family genealogy and he had a strong sense of place and identification with Wise County. However, he had traveled some and had lived with his family outside of Wise County for several years, working at a number of different jobs in Kentucky, West Virginia, Arkansas, and Missouri. These experiences combined with his nation-wide correspondence on genealogy and folklore and with the wide range of his reading to give Adams a perspective that permitted him to deal with his traditional heritage in a way that other members of his community could not. Unfortunately, Adams was never able to develop the contacts or to obtain the resources available in the wider sphere that might have permitted him to write the book he wanted to see written on Wise County—its history and folklore.

* * *

While acknowledging Chase's interest in other folklore material, it still appears that, from the beginning of the Wise County project, he was more interested in Jack tales than in anything else. And although Adams had collected six Jack tales before Chase came into the County, with Chase's focus on the tales and with firm instructions from their supervisors to give Chase whatever help he asked for, Adams and Hylton collected eighteen more Jack tales in the five months following Chase's initial visit. Ultimately twenty-eight Jack tale variants (nineteen separate tales) were collected. Adams collected twenty-four; Hylton three; and Chase one according to the headings on the actual material that was turned in and that survived to the present time. An undated list of ninety-nine tales to be used in the Wise County book includes about thirty Jack tales but this list, prepared by Chase, does not agree with the figures given above. It attributes thirteen Jack tales to Chase; fourteen to Adams; and none to Hylton.[37]

In retrospect it seems likely that Chase was never all that committed to a Wise County folklore book and that his interests lay primarily with Jack tales and his own publications and performances. While he was ostensibly working on the Wise County book for the Virginia Writers' Project from September 1941 to June 1942 he completed his book, *The Jack Tales* and in it he included, in whole or part, eleven Jack tale variants from Wise County—most of which had been listed in outlines as part of the proposed Wise County folklore book. His second book, *Grandfather Tales*, in 1948 included at least fourteen more tales (one Jack tale) from Wise County, and *American Folk Tales and Songs*, in 1956, added another nine tales to the list—including four more Jack tales.

Furthermore, in *Grandfather Tales* Chase incorporated some of the contextual material he had devised for the Wise County book and he utilized the fictionalized character of "Tom Hunt" which he had created as a persona to unify the disparate materials that were to be in the Wise County book. So, although the Wise County book was never published as proposed, a substantial amount of what was to be its content ended up in

James Taylor Adams conducted a voluminous correspondence on Adams family genealogy. Shown here is the library he built in 1952 near his house in Big Laurel, Virginia. Photo from the James Taylor Adams Papers, John Cook Wyllie Library, Clinch Valley College, Wise, Virginia.

The Adams Family Library in 1987. Photo by Charles L. Perdue, Jr.

Chase's books.[38]

Both Hylton and Adams were aware that Chase was producing *The Jack Tales* but several letters in the James Taylor Adams Papers hint at considerable dissatisfaction over the publication of the book—perhaps dissatisfaction that material slated for the Wise County book was included. There was also some bad feeling in regard to the way that credit was given (or not given) to various individuals. In 1953, only about a year before his death, Adams would look back and say:

The late Gaines Kilgore was the most famous taleteller Wise
County has ever produced...His fame was such that, when
Richard Chase published his "Jack Tales," a few years ago, most of
which had been recorded from Gaines, everybody around Wise and
Big Laurel referred to the work as Gaines Kilgore's book.[39]

Carriere, whose review of *The Jack Tales* was referred to earlier, knew that Chase had collated and edited the Jack tales and he said this of the material:

In order to make it appeal to a larger public, [Chase] has retold in
part the stories, taking the best of several tellings and incorporating
the best of all the material collected into one complete story. Yet,
his Jack tales reflect the true spirit of American folklore as it exists
in the Southern Appalachians; he has been careful to keep the
idiom throughout and not to introduce any episode which was not
in the versions heard from the [informants].

We still do not have original versions of the tales Chase collected from the Wards and others in North Carolina but with the rare texts of the twenty-eight Wise County Jack tales now in hand, it may be possible to make a few tentative statements regarding Chase's changes.

If Chase had stuck to merely editing one version of a tale the task might be easier. But he generally combined elements from as many versions of each tale as he could find and some of the published tales were collated from as many as seven different versions. Chase admitted in a letter to Adams in July, 1943 that his copies and files were, at that time, so worked over that he, himself, could not tell just where all or parts of various texts had come from.[40]

As an exception to this we might take a look at the tale, "Soldier Jack," which was edited almost entirely from one version collected by Adams from Gaines Kilgore of Wise County [Tale No. 17 here]. Although Chase retained the essentials of the tale he altered some of the motifs rather dramatically. For example, in Adams's text Jack is given a magic sack and a magic glass because of his kindness to a beggar. Jack captures an old Devil and three little Devils in his sack and keeps them there for a couple of months as punishment. Then he turns them loose and they run off home. In *The Jack Tales*, Chase has the Devils hammered to ashes on a blacksmith's anvil.

It appears that Chase simply learned Adams's version of Gaines Kilgore's tale and then retold it in his own words, and contrary to Carriere's assessment, freely introduced elements which were not present in the original. Chase, himself, tells how he creates a tale text:

About this rich and full quality that should go into any editing of this oral stuff:—The N.C. "Jack & the Giants" was quite a skinny tale at the first recording. After hearing Mr. Ward tell it again when we had a gang of kids and folks around us, it filled out considerably. But after hearing Ben Hicks, Miles Ward, and [blank] Hicks tell it, it became interesting; and after I had *told* [emphasis in original] it a few times myself it really came to life. Having gone through this telling-listening process so much with the N.C. tradition now I can do it as a [blank], but I do need a number of variants. Two or three of the Wise tales already edited, will have to be done again to enrich them with elements that were scanty, or even missing in the one version . . . I worked from.[41]

Given this evolutionary and idiosyncratic method of creating tale texts, it would appear to be impossible to ever discover all the changes made by Chase.

In a letter to Herbert Halpert dated June 8, 1942, Chase says:

I have tried to stick to my American sources in all matters of style

James Taylor Adams shown on the porch of his house in Big Laurel, Virginia, shortly before his death in 1954. Photo in the James Taylor Adams Papers, John Cook Wyllie Library, Clinch Valley College, Wise, Virginia.

The Adams house in 1987. Photo by Charles L. Perdue, Jr.

and collated each tale out of this native stuff. Only once, I think, have I inserted something from older sources...the singing a bowl full -of lies- mentioned in my letter to Dr. [Stith] Thompson. Sometimes this collation works out to be the *regular* pattern of the TYPE although only scraps of the pattern were known to my separate informants. (Is this an instinct which I have acquired?!)[42]

In some cases Chase made changes he felt were necessary for a particular audience:

I will, of course, have to change the going-to-bed incidents in adapting the tale [JACK AND KING MOROCK] for young readers edition. [Compare the version presented here (6-A) with Chase's version in *The Jack Tales*.][43]

In this same tale Chase also substituted a "big thorny bresh thicket" for the stable full of manure in which Jack had to search for a lost ring.

Richard Chase was not an academic folklorist and made no claims to be such. On the contrary, he proclaimed his lack of patience with and his independence from the discipline required by such pursuit. As he said in a letter to folklorist Herbert Halpert:

I've been trying to work on this appendix copy all afternoon. I'm afraid I'm not the type! It gives me a bad headache. As you know, my interest in all this folk stuff is rather more on the enjoyment side than on the academic.[44]

Chase's interest in collecting tales seems to have resided more in his urgency to get down the basic construct of the story rather than in accurately transcribing an informant's tale. A comparison of the versions of JACK AND THE BULL collected by both Adams (Tale No. 3-B) and Chase (Tale No. 3-C) from the same informant at the same time reveals their different approaches to the same material. Chase's rather cryptic version is two and a half pages shorter than Adams's text. While Chase's version may not accurately represent the informant's performance, it is adequate as a script to be expanded and elaborated in subsequent tellings and/or re-writings by Chase as he himself described previously.

The blame for failing to preserve the field collected material and to provide for the historical record is shared by Chase and—insofar as the Wise County material is concerned—by members of the Virginia Writers' Project staff in Richmond who failed to adequately protect the cultural documents put in their care. In the case of the North Carolina material, accurate field recorded texts may never have existed, although there is some indication to the contrary. If they did exist, they likely met the same fate as the Virginia texts given to Chase by Writers' Project workers.

The presentation of these surviving Jack tale texts from Virginia, combined with such information as that which has been provided here on Chase's creative collaboration with his (and Adams's and Hylton's) informants, may give us a better understanding of the creative process involved in the production of Chase's published works. It also allows us to more accurately assess their value and place in Jack tale scholarship.

More importantly, this case reminds us of the complex, and usually inequitable, relationships that are involved in contacts between traditional cultural groups and outside agents of mainstream culture. And it shows how these relationships can be further complicated through the impact of a single, persistent individual with sufficient personal conceit and need for self-promotion, or with a sense of mission—whether it be concerned with souls or with music or with folktales.

NOTES

JTA Papers are located in the Archive, John Cook Wyllie Library, Clinch Valley College, Wise, Virginia.

File 9829 and **File 1547** are located in the Manuscripts Department, Alderman Library, University of Virginia, Charlottesville.

1. The research upon which this article is based was supported by Grant Number RS-20373-83 from the National Endowment for the Humanities, jointly awarded to Charles L. Perdue, Jr., and to Nancy J. Martin-Perdue.
2. Leonard W. Roberts, *Old Greasybeard: Tales from the Cumberland Gap* (Detroit: Folklore Associates, 1969) 21.
3. Elizabeth Copeland Norfleet, *Blue Ridge School: Samaritans of the Mountains* (Orange, VA: Green Publishers, Inc., ca. 1982) 76.
4. Rev. Dr. Joseph Doddridge, *Notes on the Settlement and Indian Wars, of the Western Parts of Virginia & Pennsylvania, from the year 1763 until the year 1783 inclusive, together with a view of the state of society and manners of the first settlers of the western country* (Wellsburgh, VA: [now W. VA] printed at the office of the *Gazette* for the author, 1824) 159.
5. We talked to several people in places where Chase lived and worked and there was general agreement as to the comments made here. Chase, in fact, spent some time as "Folklorist-in-Residence" at Lenoir Rhyne College in Hickory, North Carolina.
6. Chase to Adams, 4 July 1942, JTA Papers, Box 47; Chase to Adams, 4 June [1943], JTA Papers, Box 47.
7. Information on Chase's early activities is based on an interview with him conducted on 8 November 1984 by the author and Nancy J. Martin-Perdue; and on a transcription of a talk made by Chase in 1962, copy obtained courtesy of Charles Alan Watkins, Director of the Appalachian Cultural Center, Appalachian State University.
8. Maud Karpeles, editor, *English Folk Songs from the Southern Appalachians,* Collected by Cecil J. Sharp (London: Oxford University Press, 1932) xxxvi.
9. At Marietta Johnson's school at Fairhope, "Old English country, Morris, and sword dancing were introduced in the teens, and under Charles Rabold's leadership in the twenties English folk dancing became one of the school's most prominent identifying features." For more information on the Fair Hope community and Marietta Johnson's school see, Paul M. Gaston, *Women of Fair Hope* (Athens: The University of Georgia Press, 1984) (99 for above quote).
10. Information on the Institute of Folk Music is included with a letter dated 9 November 1934 from Chase to Prof. Arthur Kyle Davis, Jr., at the University of Virginia. In A.K. Davis Papers, File 9829, Box 6.

11. For a discussion of Chase's role at White Top and the general background and history of the festival, see David E. Whisnant, *All That is Native and Fine: The Politics of Culture in an American Region* (Chapel Hill: University of North Carolina Press, 1984). It is not clear whether Chase worked full time for the Recreation Division or simply took occasional, short-term assignments.

12. See *Southern Folklore Quarterly*, Vol. I, No. 1 (March 1937); Vol. I, No. 4 (December 1937); Vol II, No. 3 (September 1938); Vol. II, No. 4 (December 1938); Vol. III, No. 1 (March 1939); Vol. V, No. 3 (September 1941). See also Chase's article, "The Origin of 'The Jack Tales'," SFQ Vol. III, No. 2 (September 1939).

13. National Archives, RG 69, State Series, 651.36-Virginia.

14. Ray to Chase, 29 March 1939, and Ray to Robert B. Bradford, Acting Director, Recreation Section, Professional and Services Division, 11 April 1939, National Archives, ibid.

15. Information on Adams is from his own write-up dated 20 April 1942, in File 1547, Box 15.

16. Chase to Adams, 15 March 1940, JTA Papers, Box 47-C (II), letters from Richard Chase; and Chase to Adams, 25 October 1940, JTA Papers. The letters from R.M. Ward to JTA that survive in Adams' papers are dated between 2 May 1940 and 15 December 1940. They indicate that Ward was a collector of "old folk songs" and, apparently, tales and this is a facet of Ward's history that needs further investigation. The question of how much of his repertoire came from his family and how much was collected by mail is beyond the scope of this article.

17. Chase to Adams, 19 September 1941, JTA Papers, Box 47; Robert W. Ehrman to Adams, 15 November 1941, File 1547, Box 15, Folder 3.

18. Chase to Richardson, 16 October 1941; and Adams to Richardson, 17 October 1941, File 1547, Box 15, Folder 3.

19. Adams to Richardson, ibid.

20. Sizer's comments included in a letter from Robert W. Ehrman to Adams, 15 November 1941, File 1547.

21. Index of American Design Manual, WPA Technical Series, Art Circular No. 3, 3 November 1938, p. 1.

22. Some of this material is in the Archives Branch of the Virginia State Library, Richmond, WPA-FWP Box 256; and some is scattered through several boxes of the JTA Papers.

23. Chase to Adams, 19 September 1941, JTA Papers, Box 47.

24. Chase to Adams, 8 October 1941, JTA Papers.

25. Sizer to Adams, 28 February 1942, File 1547, Box 15, Folder 3.

26. Both James M. Hylton and Emory L. Hamilton contributed much material to the volume of folklore collected in Wise County but Adams played a much larger role in that he was more seriously and more perma-

nently interested in Wise County folklore and he was also the local Supervisor for Hylton and Hamilton.

27. "Folklore Finders-Song," written by Adams, dated 20 April 1942, File 1547, Box 15.

28. Ibid.

29. Generally, on the topics in this paragraph, see Ronald D. Eller, *Miners, Millhands, and Mountaineers: Industrialization of the Appalachian South, 1880-1930* (Knoxville: The University of Tennessee Press, 1982); Luther F. Addington, *The Story of Wise County (Virginia)* (Wise: Centennial Committee and School Board of Wise County, Virginia, 1956); and Ronald L. Heinemann, *Depression and New Deal in Virginia: The Enduring Dominion* (Charlottesville: The University Press of Virginia, 1983).

30. "Folklore of Southwest Virginia," James Taylor Adams and Emory L. Hamilton, 17 May 1939, File 1547, Box 15.

31. "Folklore Finders-Song," written by Adams, dated 20 April 1942, File 1547, Box 15.

32. "Folklore of Southwest Virginia," cited above.

33. From Adams's introductory notes to tale No. 6-A, JACK AND OLD KING MOROCK.

34. "A Field Worker's Finder for Traditional Tales," James Taylor Adams, n.d., File 1547, Box 14.

35. James Taylor Adams, *Death in the Dark: A Collection of Factual Ballads of American Mine Disasters, with Historical Notes* (Big Laurel, VA: Adams-Mullins Press, 1941; reprinted by Folcroft Library Editions, 1976, n.p.)

36. Numerous examples of these stories are to be found in several boxes of the James Taylor Adams Papers.

37. The list of 99 tales is in JTA Papers, Box 82. There are three tales attributed to Adams that we have not been able to locate: FOOL JACK AND THE TALKING CROW, collected from R. Hammond; JACK AND THE BLACK KETTLE, from Leonard Carter; and JACK AND THE ROGUES, from Elisha Rasnik.

38. Richard Chase, *The Jack Tales*, appendix by Herbert Halpert, illustrated by Berkeley Williams, Jr. (Cambridge, MA: Houghton Mifflin Company, 1949 (orig. 1943); *Grandfather Tales*, illustrated by Berkeley Williams, Jr. (Cambridge, MA: Houghton Mifflin Company, 1948); and *American Folk Tales and Songs* (New York: The New American Library, 1956).

39. JTA Papers, WPA Box 24, undated but with material from 1953.

40. Chase to Adams, 31 July [?] 1943, JTA Papers.

41. Chase to Richardson, 16 October 1941, File 1547, Box 15, Folder 3.

42. JTA Papers, Box 82.

43. Taken from some notes on the Wise County book, 1 June 1942, WPA-VWP Box 256, Folder 8, Archives Branch, Virginia State Library, Richmond.

44. Chase to Halpert, 8 June 1942, JTA Papers, Box 82.

Appendix

BACKGROUND ON THE PROJECTS

In the depths of the Great Depression some forty-five percent of the American work force was unemployed. Blue collar workers were affected the most but as the Depression wore on more and more professional people found themselves joining the ranks of the jobless.

There had been cultural projects employing such professionals—musicians, actors, artists, and writers—in some of the states, but a national program could not be undertaken without federal organization, administration, and control. With the establishment of the Works Progress Administration on May 6, 1935, such work-relief became possible. On August 2, 1935, the announcement was made that the federal government would sponsor nation-wide projects employing persons on relief who were qualified in the fields of art, music, drama, and writing.

Work on the Federal Writers' Project in Virginia began officially on October 28, 1935, when Dr. H. J. Eckenrode, a historian, was hired as state director on a part-time basis—not to exceed twelve days per month. Unfortunately, Eckenrode had many interests and other obligations in Virginia, so that very little work of substance was carried out under his supervision. He was replaced by full-time state director Eudora Ramsay Richardson on March 9, 1937. Mrs. Richardson reorganized the Virginia office and began a fruitful five years of research and publication activity.

During the life of the Virginia project more than 185 workers were employed around the state in the Project's various activities. Ultimately, the Project published 8,500 pages of material and left a legacy of about 90 linear feet of research data, life histories, social-ethnic studies, ex-slave interviews, newspaper clippings, photographs, and folklore and folksongs (see Notes for location of this material). The Virginia Writers' Project closed its doors in late June, 1942.

Although the Federal Art Project was established in October of 1935, the Virginia Art Project did not officially begin until February 19, 1936, with the appointment of Miss Adele Clark as the state director—a position she held until the Project closed on June 18, 1942. A few artists had been working for the WPA in late 1935 and early 1936 making pen and ink drawings for use in publications of the Virginia Conservation Commission, but they were not employed by the VAP. Within a month after Miss Clark began work there were eleven art projects in the state employing twenty-six people.

The VAP workers established art galleries, put on exhibitions, gave gallery talks and lectures, painted portraits and still lifes, constructed dioramas, and participated in the Index of American Design program. The Project allocated many of its products to state and federal institutions and agencies but retained some 200 oil and water color paintings at the time of its close.

The Index of American Design program was conducted within the Federal Art Project. Some 15,000 water color plates of traditional and popular artifacts were produced. According to the 1938 Index Manual, the main purpose of these was to make available "usable source records of this material to artists, designers, manufacturers, museums, libraries, and art schools." Initially, Ruth Reeves was the IAD national coordinator; C. Adolph Glassgold held that position from the spring of 1936 to mid-1940; and he was succeeded by Benjamin Knotts.

The Virginia Art Project produced about 200 plates for the Index. Most of these are currently housed in the National Gallery in Washington, DC. However, a few plates remain at the Valentine Museum in Richmond, Virginia, and perhaps in other locations. Some of the illustrative material in this book is taken from the Virginia plates.